The Way of the Dog

A NOVEL

Sam Savage

COFFEE HOUSE PRESS
MINNEAPOLIS :: 2013

COFFEE HOUSE PRESS books are available to the trade through our primary distributor, Consortium Book Sales & Distribution, cbsd.com or (800) 283-3572. For personal orders, catalogs, or other information, write to: info@coffeehousepress.org.

Coffee House Press is a nonprofit literary publishing house. Support from private foundations, corporate giving programs, government programs, and generous individuals helps make the publication of our books possible. We gratefully acknowledge their support in detail in the back of this book.

Good books are brewing at coffeehousepress.org

LIBRARY OF CONGRESS CIP INFORMATION
Savage, Sam, 1940–
The way of the dog : a novel / by Sam Savage.
p. cm.
ISBN 978-1-56689-312-1 (alk. paper)
I. Title.
PS3619.A84W39 2013
813´.6—DC23
2011046604

1 3 5 7 9 8 6 4 2
FIRST EDITION | FIRST PRINTING
PRINTED IN THE UNITED STATES

An excerpt from this work was first published in the *Paris Review* (Issue 202, Fall 2012) under the title "The Meininger Nude."

THE WAY OF THE DOG

I had a most marvellous piece of luck. I died.

—JOHN BERRYMAN

I am going to stop now. A few loose threads to cut, some bits and pieces to gather up and label, so people will know, and then I stop.

I had a little dog. We went through the world together for as long as he lasted, through the world this way and that, just to be going. At the end he had grown so weak I had to prod him onward with my shoe. He is buried somewhere. His name was Roy. I miss him.

I am not well.

The woman who lives across the street is not well, I think. She looks dejected, downcast. She is not well psychologically, I think. I think she is a kept woman. They keep her because she is ill.

The dog didn't reach halfway up my shin, unless he jumped up against my leg, which he would do when he was young, when he would first see me in the morning or when I would come back after an absence. Coming back after a long absence, like a traveler approaching his natal village after many years. Kidnapped by pirates, he says, though no one believes him. Sweetheart married and fat, parents dead, he can't remember what it was he had set out to find. He can't think of a reason to leave again, so he stays on in the village until he dies, an old man, childless, wifeless, who has spent his afternoons telling the same old stories.

The neighbor was standing in the yard looking down at some flowers when her husband left for work this morning. He backed the car out of the driveway, rolling it right past her. Her illness has cast a pall over the family. It has stunted her children, who are large, handsome, but stunted emotionally. It shows in their expressions, their body language. They are neat, well groomed, as if they had stepped out of a clothing catalogue, in their rigid adherence to the codes of their milieu. In their ordinariness, their normalcy, they strike me as fanatics. A husband and three teenage sons. Summer evenings they all four shoot hoops in the driveway. If she comes out of the house, walking past them on her way to put something in the trash, they stop playing and stand silently by until she is back inside. Eyes downcast, face drawn, she seems drowned, submerged. In the evening the husband and sons return from work, school, or play to a house in which the venetian blinds on the windows are tilted shut. She is inside, huddled, her gaze turned inward. They move around her, giving her berth, but they don't acknowledge her illness even to themselves, even as they go from room to room twisting the rods that open the blinds.

There are other things. Turning in bed I see other things across the street, portions of several houses, a slice of sky, electric poles, a tree with large leaves, a catalpa. It blooms every June, big clusters of white flowers that bedeck the tree briefly and fall off and cover the sidewalk entirely. I see most of a gigantic elm. I can't see the top of the elm from the bed but know that it canopies above the roof of a yellow bungalow. In that house live a very tall woman and an even taller man, who sally forth with black briefcases five mornings a week and dress up in matching red-and-black logo-spattered spandex to ride bicycles, lean and silver, on Sundays. I don't know their names. We have never spoken. I think of them as the tall people.

Happy people, I have been thinking lately, sitting here at the window, are convivial by nature. They recognize one another by subtle signs. This neighborhood is full of them. On weekends they cluster and bunch in backyards and parks, smiling and wagging like dogs.

In the great prenatal sorting of souls I stumbled into the wrong species, I have been thinking. I was destined for something smaller, meaner, more solitary—a vile little insect, perhaps, like the character in Kafka's great story, who wakes up one morning and discovers he has been transformed into a big cockroach. Of course "deep down" he was that all along, and one day he wakes up and knows it.

I have learned it gradually. A long descent into vileness.

Scaling desiccated skin of snake, bloated belly of toad, fleshless legs of bird, smell of goat, face of camel, mind of berserk elk pulled down by wolves. A hobbler, a foot-dragger, stumbling on cracks in the sidewalk.

I have a gun.

Hours, days, entire weeks pass without pain. For the most part I waste them in sleep; sometimes I sleep twenty hours a day. Otherwise I look out the window, eager to witness every event in this quiet neighborhood, or hobble down to the river, using a stick, or sit about and tell myself stories.

The same old stories, always about "the road of life," the man who sets out on the road of life full of hope and promise and stumbles off it into a dark wood, becomes lost in thick undergrowth, skin ripped by brambles, until finally, lurching about in the darkness, he falls down a ravine, lies sprawled in the dry leaves and branches at the bottom, barely twitching, and so forth.

Diseases could be named, they have been named, I am not going to name them. This is not about diseases. Unless thoughts of death are a disease.

Roy didn't think about death, he wagged his way up to it.

This is about scraps, about scraps of paper that won't fit together. This is about litter.

I, Harold Nivenson . . .

In the beginning it was 5 x 8 index cards arranged in a steel index-card box. Later it was 3 x 5 index cards arranged in a fiberboard index-card box. There were several boxes, at different times, several steel boxes followed by several fiberboard boxes. Months ago, shortly after Roy died, when I had stopped going about as I used to, I ran out of 3 x 5 cards. I make do with ordinary typing paper now. I fold a sheet three times, then tear along the folds, making eight 4¼ x 2¾ slips that I carry in my pocket, keep in a box, or just throw away.

When I empty my pockets at night, I take the slips that have not been written on and stack them on the window ledge near the bed, where I can reach them if there is something to jot down. I used to put the others, the ones containing the day's scribbles, in the cardboard box under the bed. Lately I have taken to throwing those away. It was after Roy died that I started throwing them away.

I have gone from a professionally manufactured index-card system to a homemade amateur system, which is not a system at all but just a stacking arrangement, a pile or even a boxful.

On the rare occasions that my scrawl runs on to a second or even a third, fourth, and fifth card or slip, I fasten them together with a paper clip, forming a sheaf or, more rarely still, a booklet.

I don't know how long this has been going on. I don't remember when Roy died. I thought it was last fall, but it might have been the fall before that. Two men came to move my bed down to the parlor—that was last fall. So it was the fall before that. It is an antique iron bed. They put it where the sofa used to be. Now the sofa stands by itself in the middle of the room.

My lair, as I think of it now, consists of this room (the so-called parlor), a "studio" across the wide entrance hall, a dining room, a small "study," a kitchen with adjacent scullery, and a screen porch accessed through a door in the kitchen. Upstairs are two big bedrooms, two smaller bedrooms, and a bath. The third floor, under the roof, holds a dormered attic that runs the length of the house, with exposed rough-hewn rafters. The bath is bigger than the smaller bedrooms; the plumbing is ancient. There was a bathroom downstairs until the floor rotted through. At the front entrance is a vestibule. Benches with hinged lids line the sides of the vestibule, and there are coat hooks on the walls above the benches. I don't know whose coats are on the hooks. Hats as well.

I have pushed an armchair—a red velvet wing chair with matching ottoman—over next to a large window adjacent to my bed. From here I look out upon the small world that I have come to think of as mine. I have come to feel this chair as the center of the house. From here I make journeys, treks, painful forays, into the outer reaches, the bedrooms upstairs, the bathroom, the porch, sometimes out into the little yard in back.

On sunny days the big south-facing windows make this a bright room. At night it is dim and almost unbearably depressing. What lights there are—six tiny candle-flame bulbs in a brass chandelier, a standing lamp in a corner behind a second, leather armchair where I used to sit and read—make only feeble headway against the high, deep-blue ceiling receding into shadow above the chandelier, the uniform *beige* of the wallpaper. The large dining room, through an arched doorway, is papered in marbled Venetian red and is even more depressing than this one. I think of it as the *melancholy* room.

I could, of course, turn on the frame lights above the paintings. The room would be brighter then, but unbearable in a different way. The oppressive *proximity* of so many illuminated paintings pressing in upon me from all sides would make it a completely *impossible* room.

I shit and piss in a yellow plastic bucket that I keep under the bed and cover with a dinner plate when not in use. Some days, if I am feeling sprier than some other days, I haul the bucket upstairs and dump it out in the toilet. Otherwise I empty it in the sink in the kitchen and use a wooden spoon to force the stuff down through the drain sieve.

I used to shit in the bucket only when I was taken by surprise. Once I had to shit on the stairs, hanging on to the banister, taken by surprise. That was a phase, of dark thoughts and relaxed bowels. I am confident it is behind me now.

Roy was a tidy animal. When I was not able to take him out anymore he learned to shit in the basement, always in the same corner. I would do the same except that the stairs going down there are just as numerous and steep as the ones going to the second floor.

A small gingko tree stands in front of the house, and there is a streetlight on an electric pole across the way. When I have turned off at night a pale trapezoidal window lies across my bed, and in that window, if there is a breeze, leaf shadows move in ghostly silence. I hold out my hands, the leaves move over them, and it is eerie that I can't feel them.

I can't see Professor Diamond's house from my chair. For that I have to stand and place my right cheek against the window casing. From that position I can see most of a large elaborately laced Victorian house artfully painted in pink and blue. I am not comfortable spending a lot of time in that position, so she comes and goes unobserved for the most part.

Professor Diamond possesses a thin mouth, prominent nose, deep-set eyes, black hair pulled back severely and tied in a bun, long neck, body of Venus aging. Her face is sculpted, handsome, and predatory. "Aquiline," I suppose. She is not as old as I am.

My house and Diamond's house are the largest on our street, which runs uphill five blocks to the avenue, to the

Sunday bells of Saint Stephen's Catholic church and the feudal towers of the YMCA, and down three blocks to the park, with only a single traffic light. A cyclist who catches that on green can roll the length of the street, from avenue to park, without pedaling.

Standing by the railroad tracks at the edge of the park one can look across the river to the hills beyond. In summer the buildings over there and the distant hills are smudged in gray-violet haze.

On hot summer nights I used to go down and sit in the park, hoping for a breeze off the river. Sometimes, somewhere on the other side of the river, I would see white lights above a stadium of some kind, but I was never able to find the stadium in the daytime, pick it out from the beige and gray jumble of the other buildings.

Every morning and evening, no matter the weather, I walked Roy down there, and sometimes we followed the tracks along the riverbank. Walking at the water's edge, I steered Roy away from broken glass, picking a path over the rocks. There are no more trains on those tracks.

When there were still trains, there were train horns at night. Twice in those years someone from the neighborhood lay down on the tracks and was killed by a train.

I always knew what to do while Roy was alive. A walk in the morning, a quick piss at noon, a long walk in the afternoon, supper at six, a turn around the block before bed—an agenda that was practically a life program. I never woke up with the paralyzing thought that *I had no plan*. When we were out together Roy would walk a few paces behind me, stopping now and then to lift a leg or sniff at something, then scamper to catch up, but in a larger existential sense I followed him, adapted myself to his life program.

My life followed a dog's rhythm.

They will say, "In his final years he got down on the dog's level."

When Roy died, I let myself go. Without being conscious of it happening, I lost my grip. One day was like another, one minute was like another. I was going downhill. After a couple of months I began to notice what was happening, and from that point on, from the moment I noticed, I began to actively push myself downhill. I went downhill deliberately and at an accelerating pace, actively deteriorating until I was a total wreck.

Falling, one is seized by sudden panic. One puts out a hand, clutches empty air. But as the distance to the ground closes, the panic gives way to resignation, as the imminence of the actual swells and possibility shrivels, until in the millisecond before impact, when the door to the future is slamming shut at last, one is filled with a momentary, sudden, immense boredom. *So that was life*, one thinks. One is tempted to yawn, but there is not time.

The house is filthy, more or less choked with clutter. Clothes I don't wear, books I don't read, gadgets I don't use.

They will say, "He lived in a pigsty."

I look around, at the dirt and litter: Harold Nivenson's droppings.

The average American in the course of an average lifetime produces seven thousand times his own weight in waste product, in droppings, I read somewhere. To this heap of inevitable and in that sense *natural* waste I have added my two cents in the form of thousands of scraps of paper. Tens of thousands of bits of paper stuffed in drawers and boxes. I can't open a book without paper falling out. I don't know what I was hoping for.

In the dream I am lying on my back in bed. My eyes are open. I am surprised at how dark it is, and I wonder if the streetlight is out. There seems to be something going on with my heart, I am worried about my heart, so I check my pulse. I try for a long time, but I can't detect a pulse. Someone approaches the bed, bends over, leaning close as if inspecting my face. "Help me," I say. "Help me." The figure seems not to hear and gently presses my eyelids, closing them. It moves away. I don't see it, because my eyes are closed, but I feel it moving away. It occurs to me that no sound has come from my mouth. I think, So this is what being dead is like. I am not asleep, I am immobile and conscious, and I am completely dead. I experience a sudden inrush of horror as it dawns upon me that I am going to have to stay awake "in perpetuity," that I am going to have to experience being dead forever.

The neighborhood used to be "artistic." That made it attractive to the sort of people who have come here now. It was artistic and eclectic, people said. Before that it was drab. Run-down and drab but not quite a slum. The fact that it is now a thoroughly restored neighborhood that used to be artistic makes it attractive to people like Professor Diamond, who are well-to-do, who are "financially comfortable," as they say, and also artistic and eclectic themselves.

I am not at home here. Two decades of improvement and renewal, and now I am not at home. The people I used to know, people I was almost comfortable with, have been sanitized out. The small abandoned brick factories with their tall metal-framed windows, the squat brick warehouses, even the old school buildings, have been made over into luxury studios, so-called artist-loft condominiums, into shops, galleries, and restaurants with trendy *industrial* decors. The drab, run-down houses, with their air of narrow working-class prejudice and sordid conviviality, have

THE WAY OF THE DOG

been taken over, invaded by strivers, by good-natured *pro-fessional* people, young, insecure, ambitious parents with precocious, protected children. The old, collapsing houses have been shored, restored, and refurbished, outfitted with new wings, dormers, decks, skylights, repainted in the vivid colors of the hotter nations where the people who now live in them go on vacation. The houses have received *contemporary* facelifts and been made comfortable for *just that type of person.* As more financially well-to-do people move into it, the neighborhood houses ever-fewer actual artists while becoming ever more "artistic," containing ever-more art galleries, art restaurants, and other "art outlets," while pursuing the unconscious collective aim of becoming one hundred percent artistic and one hundred percent well-to-do.

Sitting at the window lately I have noticed the same people passing at frequent intervals. They come from one direction, and a little later they appear again from the same direction, circling, it seems, or they go to the end of the block and turn around. It is *perfectly normal,* I tell myself, for people to notice a house like mine, one that stands out from the others and must look to them like an abandoned building, though they have been glancing this way more frequently lately, it occurs to me now, sitting in my armchair and looking out the window at three women who have stopped on the sidewalk across the street and are pointing in my direction, *obviously* talking about my house. It occurs to me that in this completely upscale neighborhood my house alone still stands erect. I find myself thinking of it as "flying the banner of decay." Paint peeling, soffit boards hanging loose, curling roof shingles, broken steps, a rotting three-story *hulk*, it looms as a monument to mortality, an edifying lesson on the erosions of time, a mute reproach to the vanity of home improvement.

I should have gotten out of here twenty years ago. I should have left the minute I came back, when it was still possible to get out, when I might still have made something of myself.

With everything improving around me I find myself willfully deteriorating. Despite my obvious struggles to make something of myself I have discovered that I never had any intention of making something of myself.

What I really wanted to make of myself was a wretched failure at everything.

It was not always like this. There was a time when I had the feeling I belonged here. I would come back from a trip, drop my suitcase by the door, and collapse in an armchair. Sitting in the chair I would look around and think: home at last.

Now I think of myself as "the only one left," as "the last of the old gang."

Buying this house was the greatest folly of my life. With the money that had unexpectedly come to me, that had fallen to me as a consequence of my parents' death in a freak accident, I bought the house and had it repaired and decorated the way I wanted. I put a considerable portion of my small fortune into it. The house, I thought, would be a *launching platform* for a new life.

I bought this historic house, though I never bothered to learn its actual history.

It was the end of me. I thought I was buying freedom but I was buying imprisonment. I was buying imprisonment accompanied by an illusion of freedom. I imagined that with the house "as a base," as I thought of it then, I could go and come as I pleased, free as a lark, as I phrased it, actually saying this trite phrase to myself: "Now I am free as a lark." I imagined I would be free to travel, to take off at the drop of a hat, but in fact the house *restricted* my travels, made them so difficult they became practically impossible. I stayed only because the house was here, I came back because it was here. Without the house I might still be wandering, walking along a seashore under the stars, sleeping among sheep on a hillside somewhere. Instead of travels, with the effect of broadening my horizons, my trips became periods of recuperation, periods of rest and recovery from the burden of the house.

In college I studied agronomy, geology, comparative literature, Chinese history, et cetera. I thought of pursuing each one professionally, but after a short while each was pushed aside by something else. So I did not actually give them up in the sense of giving up on them; I was still actively engaged with them when they were pushed aside and replaced by something else that suddenly struck me as more interesting. This *flightiness,* which I thought of as openness to innovation, looked to others like frivolity, but it was in fact a crippling disability. Following the road of life, as they say, I kept wandering off into the bushes. Buying this house, I see now, was a way of trapping myself, since whatever might happen in the future, here was something I was stuck with.

Sometimes I think of it as an attempt to bury myself alive.

I thought I would completely refashion the interior of the house, I thought I would put my *stamp* on it, but after eighteen months of repairs and painting I completely lost interest in that as well, and got no further in putting my stamp on it than changing the wallpaper and replacing the plain Greek Revival chimneypiece in the parlor with a marble Italian Baroque chimneypiece.

Hanging paintings on every square inch of the walls, I thought, would make my house look like the Paris house of Gertrude Stein, who had paintings covering every inch of her walls and even a portion of the ceiling. In those years Gertrude Stein's house was superior to any museum or gallery in the world if you wanted to view the best of contemporary painting. At the time I put up my paintings I saw myself as a person of exceptional taste, someone aware of genuine art trends and not easily tricked by phony intellectual art chatterers. The house did not look like an art gallery, it was too crowded to be an art gallery, it was obviously a *collector's* house, I thought. It was like a storage house for paintings. Many of these paintings I had purchased with funds from my small fortune, some had been given me by artists grateful for my support, others had been abandoned in the house by artists passing through. I thought they were advanced, groundbreaking, completely exceptional paintings, though I can see now that they are antiquated, old-fashioned, derivative *imitations* of an advanced painting style that is itself already old-fashioned and completely dated. Paintings that I don't even look at anymore, that I am incapable of seeing with fresh eyes, that have sunk into the background, blended with it, become psychologically indistinguishable from the wallpaper.

The pistol is in a box under the bed, a chrome-plated Smith & Wesson .38 Special, bought when the neighborhood was still considered a dangerous place. I bought the house, and before moving in I bought the gun.

Slowing, the newspaper lady spins a paper from her car window, into the yard across the street. Later, when the man comes back from work, he will pick it up, slipping it from the blue plastic bag as he climbs the walk to his front door. He will go inside, open the blinds, sit in an armchair by a window, and read about the catastrophic state of the planet, the repulsive so-called advance of the earth-killing human species, but it won't actually penetrate his thoughts, it will not make it impossible for him to go on living.

That they can go on doing this, that he and his *cohorts*, as I think of them, can blindly continue to live in this way, is a sign of basic good sense, of their *robust health*, I remind myself.

The adventures of a stick: I lean heavily on it until it practically groans, unless I am feeling better, in which case I thrust it in front of me with a wild stabbing gesture, bringing it down so forcefully the pavement rings, while on the days in between, neither good nor bad, I sometimes drag it on the sidewalk behind me, the drooping tail of a beaten animal.

People will say, "He dragged his stiffened right foot like a stick. Sometimes he dragged a stick as well."

They have pulled tables from all over the park and placed them end to end for a picnic under the oak trees, where some are still seated, talking, elbows in the litter, while the rest, young men and women, play touch football in an open grassy space nearby. Wide-eyed, smiling faces, easy gaits, healthy bodies, they call out to each other, jostling, hands in the air, shouting, "to me, to me." When they look in my direction, to where I am stopped on the paved walk watching, their gaze sweeps over me. Quietly beyond their shouts and cries, through the trees, the river flashes in the

April sun. I step from the path, walk in the direction of the river, down through the middle of the game, and they stop playing, they leave off and stand idly by, good-natured, chatting, while I cross the clearing along the line of scrimmage, jabbing at the ground with my stick.

As a child I was fat, plain, nearsighted, and dirty.

Do you know what it is like to be at the mercy of sadists? To be small and at the mercy of giants, who can bring a blade down and sever your head at a whim or put a filthy boot on your nape and press your face into the mire, if it amuses them? Probably not. Then you can't imagine how it was in the wood-paneled halls and fluorescent chambers of the expensive private school to which I was sentenced as a child.

Not every teacher reveled in acts of explicit cruelty and humiliation. Not all of them actually *enjoyed* parading their trembling victim in front of a tittering mob. The others, the milder, *indifferent* ones, would send you, who were at their mercy, who were fat and nearsighted and dependent on them for protection, out into the jeering yard to be stoned, to stand bewildered in the schoolyard while they stoned you. Were teachers to behave in that way today they would be thrown instantly into prison.

To this day my throat constricts, my heart pounds, I sweat and struggle to get my breath, if I so much as walk past a school building, as if I expected a large stone to come flying over the fence. Year after year I was daily at the mercy of teachers whose idiocy and incompetence were matched only by their cruelty. It is symptomatic, nothing could be more telling and symptomatic and actually damning than the fact that today I am not able to recall the face of a single one of my tormentors. I can remember the most trivial details of the various classrooms in which I was confined year after year—the color and texture of the walls, the shape and physical feel of the desks and the names and initials carved into them, the exact arrangement of the windows, the direction of the light falling through them, the precise locations of the calendar and clock—but in front of the blackboard stands a black-clothed figure (none of my teachers, I believe, actually wore black), holding in its hand the long wooden ruler with which they used to strike us repeatedly, the black-clothed shape of a person minus the face. Instead of a face it bears on its shoulders a ghoulish white oval.

They pass beneath my window every weekday morning, in little strings and clumps, the children walking to school, shouting, jostling, sometimes turning and walking backwards. My attention goes to the outlier, the straggler, the one trudging behind the others, not too close to any of them, not *with* any of them, a child alone, head down, feet dragging, bowed under the weight of his book bag, shoulders hunched almost to his ears. A pasty, homely, *unattractive* child.

Of course it is possible, even likely in most cases, that happy people are only pretending, I have often thought. It is probable, viewed scientifically, that their so-called happiness is at bottom an elaborate superstructure of evasion and denial, a Darwinian survival mechanism of some sort, a genetic falsehood designed to stave off the suicide of the species. This is undeniably the case in those who seem most happy, those who have by virtue of their social or business or artistic success a vested interest in appearing to be the happiest of all, when in fact they secretly are the most miserable people. In fact the *professional* happiness of these people deprives them even of the meager solace they might otherwise derive from a public exposition of their misery. Surely there are many cases where happiness is only possible on the basis of some sort of mental illness.

Of course one is not talking now about the mass of ordinary, well-adjusted, supposedly happy individuals. One is talking about the crème de la crème of that mass, which would include people like Peter Meininger.

The news lady used to throw me a paper too, occasionally into the bushes next to the steps, from where I would have to poke it with a stick or leave it to come slowly apart in the rain. They raised the price last year, nearly doubled it, and I let the subscription lapse. I was not reading the paper anyway. Roy would shit on spread-out sheets after I stopped taking him out regularly, before he discovered the basement. A year has passed and bits of paper still cling here and there to the bushes by the steps.

I have always had a gift for sniffing out misery, antennae that can pick up the faintest reverberations of suffering, the flicker of a shadow across a face, the scarcely perceptible catch in a voice, the infinitesimal tug at the corner of a mouth. This ability, though it is hardly sympathy for the sufferers (I don't give a damn about them personally), creates a sort of bond. The fact is, they *interest* me. The woman across the street, for example, who seems ill, and who for all I care can drop dead tomorrow, *fascinates* me. Standing safely on the shore—I have no intention of diving in—I amuse myself by watching her drown.

The elation and immense relief that a released prisoner must feel when he steps from the prison door, while different in degree, are in kind like my feelings upon being released from boredom.

What is the point of minor artists? What justification, what possible *excuse*? The litter, the mountains of *waste product* churned out by so-called artists, *self*-called artists, who aren't artists at all but defilers of the idea of art. Instead of artists they should call themselves *besmirchers*.

By minor I don't mean unknown. The most famous painters today, for example, are also the most minor, just as the most famous writers are also the most insignificant writers. They are actually *minuscule* artists. It has always been like this, the insignificant and in fact inflated and empty rising naturally and even inevitably to the top and the weighty and significant sinking inevitably to the bottom, at least at the beginning, and there is nothing to be done about that.

I don't include so-called commercial artists, who are in the entertainment business and not artists at all.

When I talk of minor artists, I include myself of course.

Two slim books, two juvenile *pamphlets* written thirty years ago, that I can't open now without blushing: an essay on Balthus, a tedious, pretentious, art-critical "assessment" of Balthus—as if I could *measure* Balthus—and a collection of ostentatiously off-the-cuff "art reflections" absolutely stuffed with juvenile *poetic* prose.

I belittle them now in order to show myself superior to them, but at one time I was full of grandiose illusions.

Instead of a body of work I have an index-card habit.

I was able to live as a minor artist because of my independent fortune, my small independent fortune that let me be a minor artist for most of my life. A minor *literary* artist in my case.

I never admitted it of course, never admitted to being an artist at all. Not after the first years, when I was in fact a minor juvenile artist. Unlike other so-called artists, I never boasted of being an artist, and especially not of being a literary artist. I was a secret artist. For most of my adult life I was a collector of paintings and a concealed minor artist. I would not admit it because I could not accept the status of minor artist, what I considered the *disgrace* of the minor artist. I could have been a successful minor artist, but instead I was a failure as a major artist. I was a concealed failure as a major artist. By concealing the artist I was able to conceal the failure.

The chaos of my childhood—the mind- and soul-killing stupidity of the culture of my childhood in the fifties, the half-educated, middle-class, sanctimonious, self-satisfied culture that was at its core hollow and actually destructive of genuine talent, that hated everything that was different or intellectual or foreign, a culture that my parents and everyone I knew breathed in from the world around them, that was everywhere around them like a poison gas that they sucked into themselves with every breath—left me so damaged I must have seemed almost crazy.

I was crushed by art objects. In the presence of genuine art objects I felt small, I was made to feel small, I felt *belittled* by them. I pretended to be lifted up, even exalted, and I *was* exalted, but I was also humiliated. I could not become a successful minor artist because I was crushed by major art, I could not pursue possible art because I was crippled by *impossible* art.

I have always known that I was wounded by the culture of my childhood, that I was practically destroyed by it. I blamed it for my misfortunes, when in fact, I see now, I brought them all on myself.

Attempting to assert myself, I contemplated doing away with myself. In my puerile romantic way I thought of my death as *emblematic*. I was fascinated by great-artist suicides. By Hart Crane, for example, who called out ,"Goodbye, everybody," before leaping from the stern of a steamship. He was 270 miles north of Havana, returning from a year in Mexico, where he had written nothing. And Vachel Lindsay, who drank Lysol. His last words were, "They tried to get me—I got them first."

In reality nothing is more laughable than for a minor artist, some art cripple or useless art-product waste producer, to kill himself over his so-called art failure. In his studio perhaps, surrounded by his *mess*, by his *dreck*, by all the *detritus* in which he has invested so much of himself and that nobody will ever give a damn about.

I have known for a long time that my art tastes were outdated and ridiculously romantic. I see now that my paintings, which I collected through a decade of patient acquisition, which I thought were one hundred percent advanced, were in fact already "discards of history." I see now that they have no value, are essentially worthless daubings. If I had the physical strength I would throw them all out. I would hire a dumpster, park it out front, and toss them in. I imagine that if I really managed to do that I would feel immensely better, that I would be practically *cured*.

I am—I will be the first to admit it—the number one besmircher of them all.

It was not entirely my fault. In the beginning, and in fact for years after the beginning, decades after that, I was constantly *interrupted*. The interrupters camped in my house, eating my food, sleeping in every room, sleeping on sofas, rugs; on summer nights the porch was littered with them. There was always somebody around, underfoot. I would get up in the morning, thinking I was alone, planning to set to work that very day; I would enter the kitchen and find three or four of them sitting at the table. I fed them, housed them, gave them money in exchange for paintings. I thought of myself as an art patron, a *mécène*, while in fact I was a vulgar grubstaker. I thought of myself as the center of the art whirl, while in fact they were circling me like hyenas.

They came because of Meininger, they came from all over the world because of him. Not just from Europe—from Turkey, Israel, Brazil, Japan. Hundreds of them came during the three years he stayed at my house. Those people who were always around me, whom I actually took steps to *keep* around me, whom I constantly pandered to even when I was behaving toward them with maximum hostility, prevented me from creating anything but scraps.

The first painting I would destroy would be the most prominent painting, the Meininger *Nude in Deck Chair* that hangs on the wall above the baroque mantel. The garish way the artist has rendered the really classical nude figure, the way he situates her in the midst of the commercial trash that one can see actually *defines* her, the table covered with so-called beauty products, the water in the pool behind her that looks practically toxic, once appealed to me precisely because almost everyone else found them completely offensive. The hideous acrylic colors, the way the details of the body of the woman, this classically *beautiful* woman, are rendered in a soft and even blurred way except for her breasts and sex, which are reproduced in a photographically realist style, making them the actual *focus* of the work, making them actually *obscene*, made me consider this painting extremely daring, though I see now that it was always a completely ordinary painting, a thoroughly boring piece of juvenile art.

I never draw the shades—one is broken in any case—and anyone looking in has a perfect view of my wall of paintings. In the center, directly above the mantel, they see the huge Meininger nude. If they look in the window at night the first thing they notice is this offensive, contemptuous painting. If the frame light above it is turned on, especially when the rest of the room is dark, the painting is practically on the sidewalk.

Peter Meininger never referred to the mantel simply as a mantel or even a chimneypiece. When he spoke of it, it was always the *Nivenson* mantel. The electric bill, he might say, is on the Nivenson mantel. He did this, I understood, to call attention to my foolish *waste* of thousands of dollars.

The woman in the Meininger nude, surrounded by plastic trash, holds a silver bell, a small silver dinner bell clasped between thumb and forefinger as if she is about to make it ring, as if she is about to summon a servant. The hard, even scornful expression on the model's face, her posture in the deck chair, the position of the legs, the hand—Meininger wanted to call up images of Manet's *Olympia*, to overlay the nineteenth-century *whore* on this modern American *housewife*.

In order not to see the painting when I am in this room, which is almost all the time, I would have to shut my eyes. Even sitting in the wing chair facing the window, my back to the mantel, I see it reflected in the darkened panes.

Moll is back, arriving in the night. Thinking about Meininger, and she turns up like a bad penny.

I open my eyes. She has switched on the lamp in the kitchen, sending a sliver of light under the door to the dining room, and is mucking stealthily about in there, hoping not to wake me. From my bed I can hear the faint rasp of drawers sliding open and closed, the muffled clap of cabinet doors, the sudden brief screech of a chair on tiles. She will be using the chair to climb on, to search on top of the cabinets, hoping I might still keep money up there.

The kitchen light blinks out. Coming through the dining room, groping in the dark, she crashes into the wheelchair, pushes it roughly aside, grunting with effort: the wheelchair's brake is set. The noise has made her apprehensive, and she holds herself still for a time. I can feel her there, rigid and immobile, a scarcely breathing tension in the air. She is letting her eyes adjust to the dark.

She comes over, crosses the creaking parlor floor, and stands by my bed, looking down, breathing heavily from her exertions with the chair, from the tension. I pretend to sleep, watch her through slits. In the light from the streetlamp, she seems bigger. Backlit by the window, her face is in darkness.

"I know you're awake," she says, her voice coming out of the darkness. I don't say anything. I keep my eyes shut, watching through slits.

I can see her dimly, rummaging at the sideboard. She pulls out drawers, slides a hand all the way to the back of each one. She lifts the lid of a little china box, pours the coins into her pocket. A moment of awkward clinking while she struggles to fit the lid back on again.

"Now go away," I say.

As if I hadn't spoken, as if she were deaf.

Turning to the stairs, hauling on the railing, she heaves herself up them. She carries something on her back, a knapsack, I imagine. A click in the hall up there, and light floods the stairwell, illuminating the dark mahogany mass of the sideboard at the bottom, ransacked drawers hanging open, a beast of many tongues. Floorboards squeak overhead, doors slam. She is not trying to be quiet anymore. A rug from the upstairs hall flaps, folds, and tumbles down the steps, collapses in an angular heap at the foot.

I lie awake a long time, listening. Water runs in the bathroom, the toilet flushes, the light clicks off in the hall, floorboards creak in the small bedroom directly above my bed.

Now I don't hear anything. An occasional car whooshes by in the street; headlights sweep the wall and ceiling. Somewhere far off a train honks and clatters. I swallow two Vicodin, drinking from a plastic milk jug, and wake in broad daylight, to the twang of a cardinal in a tree outside.

A warm sheet of sunlight lies across the bed. The room is very bright.

When Roy was alive I would wake up, go downstairs, and he would rise from his corner, come wagging. I would go to the window and look out, and I would say "Hello, world," say it aloud sometimes, to Roy, just to be saying something to him. Roy didn't care what it was. His master's voice.

She stands over me, demanding to know where the rest of the money is. I tell her she has found it all. She reaches down and pinches my thigh.

From my armchair, I hear her in the kitchen.

She brings me soup in a cup. Vegetable soup, the vegetables in small soft pieces. She sits in the armchair and watches me. She is larger, she has become *obese,* which makes her long pale eyes seem smaller. She wears a flower-patterned housedress, and one is aware of her bulk, the big sloping shoulders, the thick wrists, and the tiny dimpled hands. I hand her back the cup. I have left the peas at the bottom. I see her looking. She holds the cup level with her chin and peers down into it. I say, "I don't eat peas."

Back at the window I notice Professor Diamond rolling past, stiffly erect and helmeted on a black-fendered bike, a briefcase laced to the rear carrier by an X of bungee cord, a chrome bell on the handlebar.

Professor Diamond has written books. Among her books, she has written novels. I have not read her books. I don't know Professor Diamond. She moved in last fall, when I was not paying attention. I have passed her on the sidewalk. She doesn't recognize me as someone she knows. I know her first name is Enid.

There was an article about her in the newspaper last winter, accompanied by a photograph. It is thanks to the photograph that I know the woman living in the big Victorian house on my street is Professor Enid Diamond. It shows her with a group of students beneath a gothic archway at the university. The students are smiling, they look attentive. Diamond clutches a thin briefcase in one hand, the other is raised. She is talking, she is *holding forth*, I think, holding forth in an *authoritative* tone, it seems to me, and gesticulating. The briefcase in the photograph is thin, practically a folder, of some soft material, leather or vinyl, while the one she carries on her bicycle has a hard case, it is a hard black box with a hinged top and a latch. Professor Diamond has (at least) two briefcases. Perhaps she transports the thin leather one inside the hard plastic one, to protect it when riding her bicycle.

The cleaning is infernal. Moll has found a vacuum cleaner somewhere and drives it around the house with furious energy. And every day she discovers fresh bits of money. Fearing thieves, I divided my hoardings, hiding them in several places, and long ago forgot where the stashes were. To escape the noise, I go outside and sit on the front steps. I carry my blanket with me, wrap it around my shoulders in the early-morning chill.

Weekday mornings the neighborhood is at its most bizarre and alienating, as if someone had kicked an anthill. They pour from the nest, rushing and tumbling into the street, mandibles masticating the last crumbs of breakfast, antennae waving. They tear out of driveways. They climb into cars at the curb. They adjust their mirrors, their radios, their headsets. They file down the sidewalk toward the bus stop at the corner. Buses swoop in, doors flop open, they push inside, the doors flap shut, the buses pull away, roaring. Diesel smoke curls and drifts in the street. They are excited, grim, resigned, hopeful, in a terrible rush, burdened with backpacks, briefcases, wires hanging from their ears. Arms swinging, heads jutting, eyes locked on the future. On days like this one, when the weather is fine, they form a *happy crowd*, it seems to me, hunched in my blanket on the steps. They remind me of the happy dwarfs in the Walt Disney movie, I expect them to burst into song. Most days, I am struck by how *intense* they seem, how *eager*, how *at home* in the workday world. At those times I feel intellectually very distant from these people. I have no instinctive feeling for that world. Nothing in my past has equipped me to understand it.

Surrounded by such people I sometimes think of myself as the *last sane man*.

When I used to encounter those people—meaning people of that type—at a neighborhood get-together, some supper party or afternoon lawn party, when I was still going to those occasionally, forcing myself to attend, when I still knew a few people here, though I hated going even then, their first question, posed within minutes of meeting me, was always, "Well, and what do you *do* exactly?" Or words to that effect, as if they were actually interested in the sort of activity that occupies me for hours every day, when what they really meant was, "And where do you get your *money*?" "What is your *job*?" People of this type always imagine that the answer to this question will tell them who I am exactly, whether I am an *alien type*, in which case they will lose interest in me, or *someone like them*, in which case they will, emotionally speaking, sidle up to me. They never begin by asking me about anything that might actually say something about who I am. The question about how I make a living is the primary thing, they are compelled to ask it, compelled to define themselves, define each other, in this purely external way by whatever mind- and soul-killing activity they have been forced into by material circumstances, though less by actual material circumstances, by an actual *dearth*, than by a pervasive ideology of *accumulation*, I have always thought. They *have* to define themselves in this way or admit that what they do day in and day out is in fact going against themselves, that in fact they are actively destroying themselves in the process.

They base their identities on work, on their jobs or their professions, especially their professions, or else on their hobbies, which are themselves just forms of pseudo work. I am alone in having *no* work, I am not even *retired* from work, which means that for them I have no clear identity, no definable personality, I am disturbingly *ambiguous*. From which they infer that I am secretive and untrustworthy. When they ask, "What do you *do* exactly?" and I say, "Nothing," they don't know how to go on.

Of course I have been shirking my whole life, a life that could stand as a prime example of complete *irresponsibility*. A life of ease, really, I will be the first to admit.

Objectively considered, it is amazing that I have managed to get so little pleasure from it.

From the very beginning I found it difficult, debilitating and painful, to work for other people, with other people. As the years went by I found it increasingly difficult to work *in the vicinity* of other people, until that too became impossible. People recognized that I didn't have a crowd, and they resented me for it. They found me disturbing, because I didn't have that restraint on me. They recognized that I didn't have people around ready to put a hand on my shoulder at the last minute, whispering in my ear, urging me to think it over. Though they themselves don't think, are incapable of thinking, they sense the danger of someone whose thoughts are allowed to go on and on without check, they are made uneasy by the presence of someone who makes a habit of thinking matters all the way through to the end, to their logical rather than their emotional conclusion, who does not stop thinking at the point where he happens to feel comfortable, I have always believed. The thoughts, unchecked, either go round and round like a snake biting its tail or they shoot straight ahead like bullets, and one ends up a madman or an assassin, I think now.

The difficulty I have in being with people, the discomfort I feel in even a small crowd of people, stems from the fact that I can see into their souls, I sometimes think. At any rate I imagine I am seeing into their souls, and I suffer the consequences.

Moll lets my son in by the kitchen door—this bald, middle-aged, middle-class *gentleman* whom I inexplicably call my son, still, despite the obvious fact that were we to meet as strangers we would find nothing to talk about. When he was a child and would come here to stay for a few weeks each summer we already had nothing to talk about. They find me in my chair, a blanket pulled up to my chin. He drags the upholstered rocker over next to me. Moll sits on the bed. We talk, and he starts rocking. Small quick oscillations. He *jiggles* the chair. He catches himself, sees what he is doing and plants his feet squarely on the floor to make it stop, and two minutes later he is jiggling again. He wants me to have the paintings appraised by an art expert. He calls those people *art experts* who are actually just tax-avoidance schemers, when they are not outright auction *bid-riggers*, I tell him.

They have cooked this up together.

I call my son Alfie. His name is not really Alfie. I call him that because he looks like the Alfie in the movie of that name. Like the actor who played Alfie. I have forgotten the name of the actor, so I just think *Alfie*, knowing in my head that I mean the actor. My son's name is Sidney. His mother, whom I scarcely knew and can barely remember, named him Sidney behind my back.

Neighbors must have complained again. This morning I noticed two men on the sidewalk across the street. They stood side by side studying a paper one of them held up so they both could see, heads nearly touching: a map or even a summons, I thought. From time to time they looked over at my house, then back down at the paper. Typical city officials, building inspectors or zoning officers, functionaries of some sort, who were "verifying their data," I thought, and I drew back from the window. I sat in the leather armchair in the corner, well out of view, expecting them to hammer on my door at any moment. When I peered out again they were gone, they had vanished into thin air. Of course there was an automobile that I had failed to notice, they must have climbed into an automobile and driven off while I was waiting for the knock. The fact that they went away without knocking has done nothing to relieve my anxiety. Had they actually knocked on my door and threatened, as has happened in the past, warning me in the sternest tones of an impending fine or even, potentially, a short prison sentence, for violating some insignificant municipal ordinance, I could have dealt with that. Instead I am facing a vague threat against which I have no idea how to defend myself.

An obscure ordinance of which no one even knows the existence. There are hundreds or even thousands of such ordinances that no one in the public is aware of and that they can use against you at any point. In fact people are totally hemmed about by them, I was thinking, sitting in the armchair waiting for the men to reappear and all the while becoming more and more agitated. People follow their daily routines feeling that they are free, I thought, when in fact they are being guided by these thousands of minute ordinances. They are caught in a web of statutes, edicts, and ordinances against which they are practically helpless, since struggling against them invariably results in their becoming completely entangled. In the end they become the kind of people who can talk of nothing but their grievances, who seize every occasion to rage against the municipal authorities, who end up spending their lives at city hall and in municipal court, in fruitless struggle, until they are finally put away somewhere.

She comes in with soup. She stands by the bed, head hanging, looking down at me, thin gray hair falling over one of her pale eyes, holding the bowl while I work my legs out from under the sheets so as to sit upright on the edge of the bed, bare feet on the cold floor. I discover a long strand in the soup and hold it up for her inspection. I say, "If this were a restaurant they'd make you wear a hairnet." She says, "If this were a restaurant they'd kick you out, sitting there in nothing but your piss-stained boxers. You're not a pretty picture, you know." "Nobody's making you look," I say.

"Here," I say, "you behold a ruin that was once a man." She snorts at this and says, "Just eat your soup." I eat, while she sits in the armchair and watches. I hand her the empty bowl. "Now off to the scullery with you." She is walking away, and I throw a slice of toast, hit her in the middle of the back. You would think she would be bald by now, the quantity of hair I find.

Roy lost a lot of hair before he died. She has vacuumed the chairs and sofa, back and forth, back and forth over the upholstery, trying to get the hair off.

I dream that I am dead again. I lie naked on a steel table. In the dream I hear the word *gurney*. Even in the dream I know that this is not what a gurney is. The room is very bright, a brightness that in the dream I think of as *antiseptic*. I look up into banks of fluorescent tubes on the ceiling. The pale-green walls are of painted cinderblock. I hear the words *sickly green*. I am held down on the table by wide leather straps across my body, *like the monster Frankenstein*, I think in the dream. Lifting my head—it requires a huge effort to lift my head—I see that I have my young body back, and that it has turned a repulsive greenish color. That is because I am dead, I think. In the dream I am reminded of Mantegna's painting of the dead Christ.

Nowadays I write in block letters. I mean it to be all angular caps, but the letters are uncertain and wavy. It looks like a child's writing, but the letters are tiny. It looks like the writing of a Lilliputian child. I am going to reach a point where the scribbling is illegible even to me. I will stop before then.

The smell of incense, sweetly malodorous, descends from her room and drifts through the house. I notice it even in the kitchen.

I was standing by the bed pissing in the bucket when she banged in through the front door this afternoon, holding the gathered handles of several plastic shopping bags. She didn't say anything. She glanced in my direction and proceeded to the kitchen and banged around in there awhile. I sat down on the edge of the bed. I pulled the sheet up and wrapped it around me.

She carried the bucket upstairs, grunting, sent back the sound of flushing. I heard her stamping around in the rooms upstairs.

She comes in, walks in out of the blue, and takes over the house, as if she had never left.

She says, "I am not going to let you die like this."

Ritual guides Moll and Alfie now, the rituals of death and the family. It is a system of morality that I personally consider entirely stupid, but the fact is they have me on their conscience.

She cleans constantly, turning the house upside down, going into crevices and the backs of cupboards to get at the concealed dirt, at the filth that has hardened over time, that has become practically part of the house, and this constant *fanatical* housework has upended what was in fact a peaceful pigsty. The obvious benefit, when it comes to sanitation, of this work for which I don't pay a penny, fails to make her presence less burdensome, does not prevent the constant invasion of privacy, which means that I pay for it psychologically, in the discomfort her presence causes. Every minute that she stays in the house, even when I can't hear or see her, even when she is hidden in the room upstairs, even when she is out shopping, I am conscious of being hindered by her.

I am going to make a statement, and then I will stop. A statement of principles, beginning, "I, Harold Nivenson, wish to make a statement."

The entire justification for taking up the index-card habit once again was finally to make a statement.

I don't sleep. I doze at best. I *oscillate* between a waking state marked by anxiety, foreboding, and remorse, and a twilight state in which consciousness is not lost, but the control of consciousness is lost, when I plunge into a sink of chaotic imagery, a tumbling stream of mental fragments, nothing resembling a dream. Every few minutes I rise to the surface, like coming up for air, and sink again, drowning. I go in and out of this state for most of the night, without actually sleeping. Or else I sleep, and I dream, and the dreams are nightmares.

As long as Moll is here my sister will stay away. That is an advantage of having her here, to prevent my sister from coming as she has threatened to do at several points during the winter. She has been telephoning more frequently in recent months, it seems to me, under the guise of finding out how I am, to ascertain that I am taking care of my health, as she likes to put it, and before hanging up she threatens to come. It is always better for her to stay away. When she is here we invariably end up in a fight, which often begins the moment she steps through the door, with a remark about one of my paintings, and the longer we put it off, the longer we manage to control ourselves, the worse it eventually is, when one or the other of us is pushed to the breaking point and finally *snaps*. She is here for only a short time, and right away we begin to argue about our parents. She persists in defending them, she wants to force me to accept her completely fanciful view of them as loving, indulgent people, where I vividly recall two monsters. These entirely opposite views of our parents end up spoiling every visit, so by the time she finally leaves we are once again hating each other as we did all through our childhood and adolescence. Moll is an *inoculating virus* protecting me from the more serious infection represented by my sister. The instant she leaves, my sister will show up. She will make the long trip here in order to put her stamp on the house again, in order to *erase* Moll from the premises. She will stay a week, two weeks, moving furniture back the way she imagines it is supposed to be, on her knees cleaning, reading to me out of books we both remember from our childhood, as if we were ten years old again. And finally she will once again face the fact that we have absolutely nothing in common, that we were so different growing up we were practically members of separate families, and she will depart in tears.

My brother and sister, the two of them alternating over the years, or even working in consort, I suspect now, personally bear the entire blame for my situation, a situation that amounts to a disability, a genuine incapacity brought on by the treatment I underwent from those two. Brought on directly by them but indirectly—and because of their position, more culpably—by my parents, who did not lift a finger to stop it.

Despite everything, my parents were always buying things for me, things they hoped would keep me amused, keep me occupied and out of their hair: puzzles, musical instruments, scientific toys, frequently several at a time, my mother or father stacking a dozen boxes in their closet, taking care always to have one or two in storage as antidotes, as emergency treatment for the episodes of literally paralyzing boredom that would overtake me even at that stage, when I would become insupportable, when I would become fantastically nagging and annoying. I was extremely fond of puzzles as a child, especially jigsaw puzzles. I was pathologically fond of them, some would say. I was in fact a small jigsaw-puzzle *fanatic*. I took an insane pleasure in them, a childlike, primitive, thoroughly *religious* pleasure in an activity that was in essence a ritual reenactment of the creation of the universe from chaos, an archetypal resurrection of a shattered world. Though they were blind to most things concerning me, especially to anything that was out of the ordinary or even remotely *weird*, my parents indulged my jigsaw addiction by showering puzzles upon me.

I was still quite young when my brother or my sister, or the two of them tittering and whispering together, devised their sibling torture regime. They would manage to sequester a *single piece* from a puzzle, and hide it from me or perhaps even destroy it. They would contrive to do this no matter how carefully I guarded the puzzle, keeping it in my room and never taking my eyes off it while one of them was around. Sometimes it seemed to me they would contrive to do it even before I had opened the box. I would always hope when I began assembling a new puzzle that *this time* I would possess all the pieces, that it would be possible *this time at last* to form the complete picture shown on the lid of the box. But even as I worked on the puzzle I could never entirely banish the fear that despite my efforts they had once again made off with a piece—a piece that now for this very reason became the *essential* piece. The bare *possibility* that this had occurred would produce in my younger self an anxiety that would thoroughly destroy the pleasure I might otherwise have derived from the puzzle. The slightest problem finding a desired piece would cause me to leap to the *fatal* conclusion that this was the *very piece* they had taken, though I had no more evidence of that than a temporary difficulty locating a particular piece among hundreds of similar pieces, a difficulty that is part and parcel of puzzle making. Sometimes, having leaped to this conclusion, having been driven to it by my intense anxiety, I would be overcome by despair, the psychologically inevitable final step in the siblings' torture sequence, and in that final despairing state I could seldom resist sweeping the entire puzzle off onto the floor, the sound of the cascading pieces drowned by their howls of laughter.

The lure of puzzling was always too great, and eventually, sniffling and tear stained, I would gather up the scattered pieces and resume my work. I would continue working even though I knew with absolute certainty that they would *always* have succeeded in removing the essential piece. With pigheaded obstinacy, perhaps just to spite them, I would continue to work on something that I knew was impossible to finish. And indeed I always ended up "completing" a puzzle from which a single piece was missing. After a while, constantly working at something impossible to finish, I came to see this as the normal course of events. In place of the *impossible goal* I put the *hopeless project,* and this now became the real concealed aim of my actions. A person looking at one of my "completed" puzzles would scarcely notice the pictured scene. That scene, the ostensible goal of the puzzle, would in a sense have disappeared, completely destroyed by the absence of the essential piece, an absence that had now become *glaring*. All eyes would fly to the hole in the puzzle. In place of a fully completed picture of a busy barnyard or thrilling naval battle, for example, that person would see a fully assembled *representation of incompleteness*, a perfect picture of failure.

The smallest member of the family, I easily became the most burdensome member. I was accused of driving the others crazy, though in fact they had already driven me crazy. Faced with my robust, competent, one hundred percent healthy brother and sister, a brother and sister who were inevitably, even *naturally* victorious, I became the awkward, incompetent, sick one, the one who was *destined* for defeat. I became, in my family and *for* my family, and ultimately for myself as well, the representation of failure.

She has been shopping and has bought, among other things—mountains of groceries, a new vacuum cleaner—a shade to replace the broken one on the window by my bed. She has found a standing fan at a yard sale. The oscillating mechanism is broken, but she has set it up so it will blow on my chair. It is cooler today. She has not turned it on.

The middle of the night, and she is still awake. I hear the television in the bedroom. She spends a lot of time looking at television. She can't sleep, or she sleeps with it on.

She spends the money Alfie has given her, money she has *extracted*, that she has practically *extorted* from him in exchange for taking me off his hands, I have to assume.

Wrapping myself in a blanket I go over and sit in the wing chair. Lights are still on across the street in the bungalow under the elm. The tall young woman is standing in the illuminated frame of an upstairs window, head bowed, talking to someone I can't see, who perhaps is stretched out on a rug or a low bed. She makes large sweeping gestures as she talks. She is *carrying on*, I think, *remonstrating* with the person lying on the bed. She glances toward the window, and stops abruptly, as if suddenly aware of my presence. Stepping to the window, she opens her arms wide and with a swift embrace draws the curtains shut. Like slamming a door in my face. One by one the lights blink off, room by room, first downstairs, then upstairs where she was standing, and each time a window goes dark I experience a small shock of abandonment.

The tall people are in bed now, in each other's arms, I think. Their lovemaking, I imagine, will be slow and languorous, giraffes coupling in the hot African night.

Envy begins in the solar plexus, climbs into the chest, the throat, gnaws with razor teeth. The ferret of impossible longing. That they should be young, and not I. Do you understand that?

In bed afterward, in the dense uncomprehending dark, I am conscious of something like a mask being pressed against my face: it is my own face, which I have drawn into a horrible grimace.

In the beginning was the wound. A psychic wound inflicted at a time when the self was still being formed, it is not reachable anymore. It was walled off a long time ago, so it would not be touched. It could not stand being touched.

Untouched, unremembered, unreachable behind the wall of the self, the wound decays, dries up, and shrivels until it is not a wound any longer but a hollow place, a howling emptiness within the brittle shell of the self.

The life struggle—the guiding principle of every thought and action—is to not fall into the hole within. The recurrent nightmare is of a man pitching backwards off a cliff, endlessly falling.

A man without a center. Unbalanced, you will say.

I would have pitched backwards years ago, but I held on to Roy.

In this neighborhood of strivers.

Thinking it over now, I am surprised at how entertaining I found watching the woman in the window, when as a matter of fact there was nothing entertaining about it. As a matter of fact this was just a quite ordinary woman silently carrying on, and I had not the slightest idea what she was saying. Obviously, the entertainment value had nothing to do with the woman or her holding forth and stemmed entirely from the fact that I was *spying*.

She flicks a roach carcass into the dustpan.

Every morning there are fresh carcasses on the kitchen floor or on the countertop. She sweeps them up or picks them up in a paper towel.

I used to just kick them aside, or knock them under the refrigerator with my stick.

They die in the night, in the middle of the kitchen floor. They are on their way somewhere when they stop and die, apparently.

Alfie is back this morning. He comes in, leading a woman by the hand, introducing her as "my wife, Janine." His third wife, she is the first with children—two preadolescent boys, shy, overweight, unappealing, who hang back in the doorway, gaping. She is bland, soft-spoken, pretty, very blonde, has nice teeth, and is much younger than he is. She walks around the room looking at the paintings, pausing in front of each one, trying to look at it like an art connoisseur, the way she imagines an art connoisseur would look at paintings. "I really like this one," she says a few times. She calls them *canvases*. One has the feeling that this is a conscious decision on her part, always to call them *canvases*.

The four of them in a row on the sofa, children in the middle. I take the rocker. It occurs to me, sitting there, that facing me in this way they have become conscious of being a family, it might be the first time this has happened to them. By confronting them in this way, a way they must experience as interrogative, even *inquisitory*, I have made them conscious of being "all in this together." The situation is uncomfortable for them, and instead of sitting there in a relaxed manner, they are all, even the children, consciously posing.

The ill woman was outside again yesterday, on the sidewalk several doors down from her own house, closer to my house. She was looking in through the window of a parked car, her face almost touching the glass. Hands up shading her eyes against the glare, she seemed to be looking at something on the backseat, she seemed frozen in that posture. I was watching her, leaning forward in my chair for a better view, when her husband came out on the porch and glanced up and down the street. He is looking for her, I found myself thinking, she has escaped again. He looked down the street and caught sight of her there bent over against the car window in that awkward frozen posture, and he came down the steps, down the sidewalk, walking in a *deliberate manner*, I thought. It occurred to me that approaching her in this calm, deliberate way was a strategy on his part. He stood next to her and bent over and put his head close to hers, he seemed to be whispering to her, while she continued to stare into the window, forehead pressed against the glass, not looking at him, possibly not even hearing him. Then he took her hand, she let him take her by the hand, and they walked back to the house together. They live in constant fear that she will wander off and do something to herself.

If someone had happened upon the scene at just that moment and seen the two of them walking back to the house hand in hand like that, that person might have thought they were a couple who had just met, perhaps a couple who, in full middle age, had managed to fall in love again.

I felt unwell and had earlier abandoned the idea of going outside or to the park, but now I took my stick and went into the street, as if stepping out for a breath of air, in my slippers. I crossed the street to the car and leaned against the window in just the way she had. But nothing was there, just a plaid lumber jacket lying on the backseat, an ordinary red-and-black wool jacket someone had tossed there carelessly, sleeve hanging off the edge, folding onto the floorboards, bent at the elbow, making the jacket seem almost human, and I could picture the ill woman's horror-stricken face looking in through the window and discovering the mutilated arm.

Even the most banal events and objects are steeped in mystery. I look out at a world that, if I think about it for more than a second, looks back at me with an expression that is completely unreadable. Did the husband *accompany* her back to the house? Did he *guide* her home? Did he *drive* her back to the house? Did he *persuade* her to go back inside? The fissure between an act and its description, between the facts and the story, is unbridgeable. There is no necessary connection between the events of a life and the lies that recount them.

Peter Meininger was a typical case. He belongs with me in the museum of typical cases. I saw the moment we met that he was on his way to becoming a failure. He was thoroughly set on becoming a failure and his entire struggle for success had just that in mind, to struggle for success in order to fail. He arrived from Munich, having abandoned his young wife and two small children, ruthlessly abandoning them without a penny, forcing her to rely on the support of her parents, whom she had always hated, parents who, I thought, were the reason she had married Peter in the first place. He let everyone know that he had come to America to make a *clean break,* in order to devote himself *absolutely* to his painting. Two days after landing, jet-lagged and exhausted, but also exhilarated, excited by his own ruthlessness and daring, he sat with me in my kitchen. We were drinking the Irish whiskey he had bought at the airport and playing chess, while he talked nonstop in a way that struck me as feverish. In the midst of our game the phone rang. Meininger's wife was calling from Munich. She was calling to say things that would make him feel awful, that would make him ashamed and make him hate himself, to paint a picture for him of the terrible conditions in which his wife and children now found themselves, whose lives he had ruined. I could hear the voice in the phone, tiny and shrill, going on and on relentlessly, while Peter listened and said scarcely a word. And then he began to cry. He didn't make a sound, while the tears rolled down his cheeks and fell on his shirt, and he didn't try to wipe them, and I am sure his wife had no idea that he was crying.

Meininger's discipline, the ruthlessness with which he swept obstacles from his path, the *self-abnegation* implicit in that ruthlessness and discipline marked him as an *art hero,* I thought at the time.

I thought at the time that he was in it for the long haul, that he was an absolutist of the spirit. It took California to turn him into an art-trend *phenomenon,* a kind of middlebrow, culture-magazine *centerfold.* Whatever his merits as a painter, he was an art-business genius, who became filthy rich with his supposedly shocking paintings. Of course I would have done the same, though not with painting, with something else. If I had not had a small independent fortune, I would have used my talents to become a shocking failure like Peter Meininger, who was forced by material circumstances to make a name for himself, a shocking literary failure in my case, a mass producer of best-selling literary waste products, for example. Meininger was forced by circumstances to fail privately as a great artist while succeeding publicly as a minor artist, a minor producer of painterly waste products that one sees everywhere in magazines and waiting rooms these days, while I was permitted by circumstances, by the fortuitous accident of a small fortune, to turn my back on the whole business, failing privately as a great artist and succeeding publicly as a minor dilettante, a man locally famous as an art appreciator and utterly unknown as a literary failure.

Empedocles killed himself by leaping into the caldron of Mount Etna. Disciples found his shoe on the rim of the crater.

Empedocles's leap into the crater was meant to prove he was a god, or, in the view of some, to trick others into believing he was a god. An apotheosis or a swindle, depending. In that ambiguity, Empedocles becomes the perfect artist.

In Dostoyevsky's *Demons,* Kirillov shoots himself, having explained to everyone that by this singular act he will prove that there is no God and that he, Kirillov, is God. Kirillov is perfectly rational and completely crazy.

Alfie sits in the rocker, *jiggling* while I talk, totally incapable of simply listening in a calm and thoughtful manner. It is torture for him to have to sit still and listen.

That is how the craziness of a family degenerates, like everything else. From my father, who was a vicious, diabolical, thoroughly concentrated *lunatic,* to my son, who is a small, repressed neurotic. It is impossible for this son to go crazy in the larger, generous *Kirillovian* sense. He could not go *mad*. It is insanity without creative force. It is like starvation, the mental starvation of a comfortably well-off, insane *tax attorney* who comes to visit his father in hopes of making that father regret having brought him into existence. He wants me to see how well things have turned out for him, but at the same time he wants me to see how bad everything is. He wants me to be proud of his achievements, and he wants me to be ashamed of having ruined his life.

He talks to me about the house. He wants me to let him fix the house, which he says he can easily afford. He won't say the word *rich*. He says "comfortably well-off." He has been giving Moll money. He is a minor artist too. He is a failed minor *escape* artist. He thought he would escape by becoming the opposite of me, the irreconcilable contradiction of his father. Whatever he set out to do it was because it was the contrary of what I would have set out to do. In the process he has made himself one hundred percent sane on the surface and seventy-five percent insane underneath. In fact the sane surface is held in place, cemented there as an unalterable *rigidity of character,* by the craziness underneath, lying there underneath as a permanent potential for a nervous breakdown.

He would like me to feel guilt, but I don't feel guilt, I feel weariness.

Hölderlin wrote a play called *The Death of Empedocles*.

But Hölderlin didn't commit suicide. He went insane instead. Büchner didn't commit suicide either. He died of typhus at the age of twenty-three. Van Gogh went crazy and then committed suicide.

Hölderlin wrote about the death of Empedocles before becoming crazy. Van Gogh did some of his best paintings after becoming crazy.

It is probable that being crazy or not being crazy has no bearing on whether the art one produces is any good or not. In my experience the producers of minor art waste products are usually one hundred percent sane.

Of course I always had money, the freedom of money. Just that *little bit* of money made it impossible for me to lead a normal life. I was set apart from the others, because I had an independent income, a *small fortune*, which I actively squandered.

My parents did not commit suicide. Their cabin cruiser was sliced in two by the destroyer USS *Keller* off the coast of Florida.

In bed, I listen to the shrill cries of children playing in the street. They have, I notice, the same excited tones as the chirping of the sparrows. A long strand of cobweb hangs from the ceiling above my bed, and in the faint draft from the open door to the kitchen it wafts and sways, causing, it seems to me, the children's voices to rise and fall. She has the radio on in there. I don't understand how anyone can listen to the radio for even fifteen minutes and not want to kill himself. It seems impossible that she can listen to the demented voices and songs for hours at a stretch, that she can even *sing along* with them. Radio and television, I have always thought, are just part of an ongoing mental-annihilation-and-suffocation process that is crushing me and everyone like me. Everyone, that is, who is not actively complicit in the annihilation, who does not have a lucrative *professional* position with the task of furthering the annihilation, making it more pervasive and crushing every day.

The insulting, aggressive, brutal, *brutalizing* advertisements on the radio and television: that people—the viewers, the listeners, the so-called mass-media consumers—permit themselves to be talked to, to be talked *at*, even shouted at, in this manner is itself the most disgusting sign, indeed the most revolting *symptom* of a disease that is destroying not just the ones who are suffering from it and actively spreading it about in the form of professionally applied contagion, but everyone else as well, people like me, who would otherwise have nothing to do with it, who would keep themselves entirely free from it.

By "people like me," of course, I mean the ones generally regarded as inveterate gripers, malcontents who deliberately, perversely, refuse to see the good in anything unless it is something they personally have invented. In other circumstances, I have always thought, such people precisely would be the healthiest and most productive people, while in this environment they have become the sickest and most useless.

Most of the people I see walking past on a regular basis, in the morning and again in the evening, going to work and coming home from work, who live in the houses up and down the street and whose faces are completely familiar to me, fail to look at my house, I have often noticed. Seldom an idle glance in my direction, and that is perfectly normal—one cannot expect them to look every time they trudge by, day in and day out, they are not municipal bureaucrats, it is not their *business* to look. But I have noticed lately that certain people, Professor Diamond chief among them, are *systematically* failing to look. My house is the most inescapable sight in the neighborhood, it is practically a tourist attraction, yet these particular people walk briskly by without turning their heads even a millimeter in this direction, having obviously made a resolution *never* to look in my direction. It seems to me, sitting at the window as they pass, that they are actually averting their eyes. Of course they know that I am at the window, they are intensely aware of this, and their refusal to look is nothing more than a primitive psycho-magical attempt to *erase* me from the picture. They pass with rapid steps, with rapidly *accelerating* steps, it seems to me, always on the opposite sidewalk, and sitting in my chair at the window I experience a strange excitement, as if my gaze were pushing them down the street. With these people, it seems to me now, I am locked in silent struggle.

Except for calls from my son and my sister, calls I have always discouraged, the phone had stopped ringing. Now it rings again, from morning to night. She spends a lot of time on the phone.

Without a word of greeting she places a bowl of cereal on the table in front of me and goes back to cleaning. I add milk from the carton and spill some of it. A small brown beetle traverses the tabletop. It encounters the milk puddle and stops. It seems to be thinking, oscillating tiny feelers. It turns and lumbers off in another direction. It moves slowly, hesitantly, like a blind thing. It seems weary. Reaching the edge of the table it waves its front legs in the air, poised above the precipice, as if feeling for something out there.

She has cleaned the stove. She has even scrubbed off the brown baked-on grease streaking the oven door. I watch her while I eat. She empties the cabinets above the counter, making maximum noise, banging cans and jars down on the countertop, slamming cabinet doors, while conducting a muttered commentary on the dirt, complaining about it, *marveling* that anyone would live in filth like this. She fills a saucepan with soapy water and puts it on the counter. She wipes the cans and jars, dipping her cloth in the water. She changes the water in the saucepan. She stands on tiptoe and scrubs the bare shelves with the cloth, then climbs on a chair to scrub the top shelf. She scrubs vigorously, the hammocks of flesh beneath her raised arms jiggle and sway. She is wearing a purple sleeveless dress that goes badly with her skin, her pale, unnaturally white skin that is now covered with reddish-pink splotches. The skin of her face, sweaty and flushed with effort, is so red, so inflamed, it looks practically *roasted*.

Sitting in my chair, I listen to her moving about overhead. She can't sleep, she says, and she goes up in the afternoon to rest. Sometimes I wake up in the middle of the night, hear the television playing softly in her room.

A fair-weather day, the fullness of spring, and they pass the house in steady procession, down the street to the little playground in the park. An hour, two hours, and the same people trudge back up it, tugging the arms of reluctant offspring, leaning stiff-armed to the carriages—women mostly, couples sometimes, rarely a man alone. They parade their progeny (or their employer's progeny) in several kinds of conveyance: enormous big-wheeled buggies, little red plastic wagons, covered trailers towed by bicycles. To accommodate multiple offspring they have double- and even triple-wide strollers that span the sidewalk like threshing machines, forcing others to step off onto the grass. There are streamlined three-wheeled racing strollers powered by the hard-muscled pistons of jogging females. A fair number of the women, I notice, also push before them gibbous bellies in various stages of tumescence in which the pupate forms of new homunculi are riding. How fermenting and fertile the world around us is, I find myself thinking. From a district of aging working-class white people drinking cheap beer on collapsing porches we have become a neighborhood of middle-class *breeders*.

The trees are in full leaf. The city's mowers have striped the park in bands of varied green. It is the *fecund* season. Birds, insects, people, microbes surely, are breeding right and left, in trees, even under the ground, in cracks. Everywhere life swarms and pullulates, and meanwhile this house, *inside* this house, feels like a *dead zone*. I stand at my window and look out at the parade of families. They live in a world of beginnings, of the first step, tooth, word, date, marriage, child. So different from a world of terminals and closures. So many ways of marking an end. I am particularly fond of the phrase: *it is curtains for him*.

We know scientifically that the "purpose" of human life, as of all life, is reproduction and death. What we don't know, don't *want* to know, is that beneath a veneer of foolish happiness our own individual lives are nothing but reproduction and death, have no point but that, we are on earth for no other reason than that. The problem is, this life of reproduction and death, if measured by the criteria and standards of significance of an even halfway civilized culture, is meaningless, completely pointless, and stupid.

She has come back with a little television for the kitchen. The idea is never to have silence or an instant without the chatter of idiotic voices. The idea is to drive me crazy. I scream at her to turn it down. She turns it slightly lower. A few minutes later it is back up again.

She helps me upstairs to the toilet. She comes into the bathroom afterward, and we stand side by side looking down at the blood and shit.

Late afternoon, and the windows were open wide, letting in sounds from the street. I lay in bed, eyes closed, and pretended to sleep. She sat in the armchair. I opened my eyes, and she had closed hers. She was moving her mouth, gnawing on her tongue.

My son comes with flowers, a bouquet of yellow roses. His wife arranges them in a vase. She tries several spots, standing back a ways and considering, before deciding to place the vase on the mantel. Obviously the roses are her idea.

He has to visit. He doesn't have the courage to just not come, and so he brings his family. They are here to make the visit into an occasion, to turn it into a superficial *social event*. Instead of painful silences we are going to have mindless chatter.

He regards the house with distaste, he has taught his family to regard it with distaste. That much is clear from the way they look at everything, the four of them sitting about the room, occupying every chair in the room, and in their boredom looking around with distaste at the paintings, as if these were somehow malevolent, as if the paintings were to blame for everything. Janine considers this house the locus of her husband's suffering, the place that originally wounded him, the source, she probably thinks in her pop-culture way, of his *primal abuse*.

It is quite possible her husband has indoctrinated her into thinking that.

He has his mother's large eyes. Eyes that expect the worse. He has been waiting his whole life for the gesture of affection that will wipe out all the wrongs of the past.

Meanwhile his wife walks around the house, appraising everything, writing it all down in her little notebook.

I walk in and find Moll at the kitchen table, staring at the little TV she has set up on the counter. Hypnotized by the television, she doesn't seem to notice me passing through. As if she were losing her mind.

She looks weary, completely worn out. She has bursts of energy, an hour or two of activity so intense it is practically *frenetic,* cleaning, cooking, digging through decades of stuff piled everywhere in the house, sorting, stacking, and all the while humming or even singing, and then she collapses, falls asleep in a chair, arms hanging at her sides. A tall, obese woman who has gone completely limp, sitting at the table staring at television. The phrase: *she's had the stuffing knocked out of her.*

I have not been able to put into words how astonishing it is to see Moll old.

They are moving furniture from a large Mayflower van parked in the street in front of a house at the end of the block. I watch them unload an enormous crescent-shaped leather sofa with matching easy chairs and a gigantic so-called *entertainment center*. They are obliged to disassemble the sofa, breaking it down into three separate pieces, each the size of an ordinary couch, in order to work it through the front door. A middle-aged couples hovers about, meddling and *supervising* the men who are moving their furniture. Now and then one or the other makes a little dart at some item being transported past them. The man addresses the movers, two burly black men and a smaller white man, with a familiarity that strikes me as false and forced, dropping his *g*'s in a completely shameless way that betrays his unease in the presence of people of a lower class, even though, I am thinking, he does not allow himself to think of people as belonging to a lower class, especially black people. He has a neat white-streaked beard and wears a Grateful Dead T-shirt and jeans. His wife flutters in and out of the house with the movers, practically stepping on their heels, hovering and interfering. The two of them strike me as typical *university* figures. A *pair* of university figures, I think, working in a department of the so-called humanities. A typical pair of shameless pretenders, who have long since lost faith in the humanities. Universities teem with such people, who in clever career moves have turned themselves into the foremost apologists and intellectual defenders of contemporary media trash culture. The university as presently constituted—*minus* those departments within it that now form a nearly self-contained scientific-technical institute, that have already effectively *quarantined* themselves from the rest—is a death trap for the mind, I have long thought. Standing across the street, watching the movers, I can picture the crescent-shaped sofa and chairs packed with upper-middle-class professional *barbarians* staring gape-mouthed at a television so big it is practically a cinema screen, just the sort of university people who are relocating, as they phrase it, to this part of town.

I think of André Breton's remark—that "the simplest surrealist act consists of going into the street, pistols in hand, and firing blindly into the crowd."

To which he adds: "Anyone who has not wanted at least once to be done with the current system of debasement and cretinism in this manner has a place reserved for him in that crowd, belly level with the barrel."

Disregarding the fact that Breton was a notorious windbag, his infamous and shocking remarks are actually the most humdrum of observations: a frank acknowledgment that in the heart of any halfway decent artist lies a murderous hatred of the so-called wider public, a huge store of resentment and loathing of the so-called *average person*, who quite rightly recognizes genuine art as inimical to himself and his life habits and who therefore *necessarily* experiences it as something unpleasant and destructive. There is of course a near-universal agreement among people in the art-supply-and-consumption business to hide this fact from the wider public, and of course the artists themselves collaborate in this obfuscation for obvious motives having to do with career enhancement and ordinary human cowardice.

André Breton was born the same year as Antonin Artaud.

It has occurred to me that I can shoot Professor Diamond off her bicycle.

In my case the idea does not spring from an innate impulse to violence. I am not conscious of any such impulse in regard to Professor Diamond. I don't imagine that in some hour of determined anguish I will, like Raskolnikov, *resolve* to shoot her, though I think it possible that I will shoot her.

Possible, but not very likely. As things stand, I find it *im*possible to say just how likely.

Like Raskolnikov I have on occasion thought of myself as an *exceptional* man.

Nor would it be out of some existentialist project to prove that "I am free." I have never believed that I am free. I am absolutely *not* free, which is why I think it possible and perhaps even *unavoidable* that I will shoot Professor Diamond.

Likeliest of all is that I am not an exceptional person and that I am simply incapable of shooting my neighbor.

Raskolnikov anguished over his murderous thoughts. I toy with mine.

If I do shoot her it will be in extremely cold blood.

I am not well.

It is possible that a so-called "mindlessly destructive act" is really an attempt by the perpetrator to rescue himself from a destructive *disease*, to wrench himself back into mental balance. After such an act, such a physical and mental *emetic*, the perpetrator, who is also the principle sufferer, returns to being a good person. In psychiatry, electroshock therapy achieves a similar effect, I believe.

I don't expect people to understand that.

Some days I find my mood in perfect harmony with Breton's statement. It *resonates* with me. And then the next day I see something, see someone, I catch a foolish smile, a moment of unreflective grace, a gesture of compassion, an old woman feeding pigeons, a mother caressing the hair of a child, and I want to throw my arms around them. Stay with me, I want to say then, Don't leave me out here alone.

I sometimes regard my life as a succession of diseases. No sooner cured of one than I was infected by another. And I was not ever really *cured* of any of them. They were pushed into remission, but I was still infected with them. I was scarred and weakened, and the ground was made fertile for a new one. The terrible thing is, each of these diseases at first impressed me as perfect health. I would become infected with a brand-new malady, and I would congratulate myself, thinking that I was well at last.

Harold Nivenson went this way, then that way, then another way altogether, and so forth, and he made a pattern of ragged zigzags down the road of life.

Just after sunrise and the spandexed giraffes are outside doing stretches on the little patch of lawn in front of their house. I sit on the edge of the bed in the new pajamas she has bought me and watch them through the window. They go through this stretching ritual before every bike ride. Despite being extremely tall they are able to bend at the waist and place both palms flat on the ground in front of them and walk their hands away from their feet, forming a wider and wider upside-down V. I watch them walk their hands back to their feet and stand like that, folded over, immobile, heads turned to face each other, talking. They straighten and look around, slim and graceful, sniffing the morning air. Maybe they smell lion. Moll comes up behind me, stands by the window. I instinctively move my arm to shield the paper from view. "Stop *staring* at people," she says, and jerks the shade down. I send it rattling back up. The couple walk to their bikes, stumping clumsily across the lawn in black biking shoes, the way people walk in front of children when they are pretending to be giants. On their bikes now, they flow down the drive and sweep into the sunlit street, wheels bright, shimmering blurs.

Moving to the chair by the window I place my bare feet in a patch of warm sunlight on the floor.

Moll has people in the kitchen. Voices of several women. Laughter. The kitchen door is shut and I catch scarcely a word.

Later, in the kitchen, I see coffee cups and crumbs. She is *entertaining* in there, receiving guests in the kitchen like a nineteenth-century *housekeeper*. They knock on the back door and she lets them into the kitchen.

From across the park, even with her back to me, I recognize Professor Diamond seated on a bench near the playground. I recognize her from the back by the long thin neck crowned by a chignon of dark hair. I make my way across the grass, steadying myself on the uneven ground with my stick. She sits at one end of the bench, an elbow on the armrest, a small blue backpack on the seat beside her. Rounding the bench I sit down at the other end. Of course she recognizes me as someone who lives on her street, and no doubt that prevents her from leaping up right away. She turns in my direction and nods curtly, without smiling, then seems to give full attention to the playground in front of us. A small girl says, "Hey, no pushing," and a boy the same size pushes and she shoots down the slide. "I'm gonna get you," the girl shouts. She races around the slide and scrambles up the ladder, has nearly reached the top when the boy lets go, swoops to the bottom, and runs off across the grass, the girl in pursuit. Sufficient time has now passed. Without looking at me again, Professor Diamond reaches for her backpack, gets up, and walks away.

This morning among the voices in the kitchen I recognize my son's. He has been coming to see her behind my back. He comes several times a week now. We are approaching the *denouement*, I find myself thinking.

Moll unwraps the package: a genuine china chamber pot with lid.

The new neighbor is standing on the steps of her house, watching us approach. She is dressed in jeans and a man's long-sleeved shirt with the cuffs turned back, shirttails reaching almost to her knees. She has a small, pleasant, worried face that is becoming pinched with age, I notice, and a great mop of red hair. She is wearing yellow latex gloves. "Nice day, isn't it?" she says, and Moll makes us stop. The woman, who does not come down from the top of her steps, tells us they are refugees. Those are the words she uses: *we are refugees*. She removes her gloves and places her hands on the stair railing, leaning over, gripping the gloves between her palms and the railing. She tells us they have been *driven out* of the area around the university, where they would prefer living, they have been chased out by people with *acres of money,* she says, who have made it unaffordable for middle-class people (she means people like herself and her husband) to continue living there, even though they are both teachers at the university. The housing situation has forced them to become *commuters,* she complains from the top of the steps. Standing on the sidewalk, half listening to Moll and the woman talking about the housing situation, I find myself thinking about how the social and cultural condition of university professors has changed in recent decades. It occurs to me that workers in the so-called humanities, people like this woman and her husband, are now basically *cultural machine operators,* day laborers in the inhuman industrial-scale manufacture of useless commentary on mass-culture products. Though I never set foot there now, I was once a university *habitué,* I was over there every day working on my Balthus pamphlet, when I was practically an *art scholar.* They think in lockstep. They all have the same humanist morality, the same liberal politics, the same barely disguised class anxiety, the same laughable faith in the value of independent inquiry and thinking for oneself. Seen strictly from the point of view of a potential flowering of intellectual diversity, nothing was gained by liberating the serfs.

I am thinking it would be best to shut the universities down and replace them with scientific-technical institutes, though I don't say those things to her.

The neighbors and I seldom speak. But when we do I am a portrait of courtesy.

She asks where we live. Looking in the direction Moll indicates, she says, "We were wondering who lived in that house."

I happen to know a great many things, still. Not things that would help toward understanding, not "wise sayings," just pointless tidbits, amusing anecdotes, intellectual garbage, and random scraps of information.

For example, that Edward Lear's mother bore twenty-one children.

That in India the Jains sweep the path in front of them in order not to crush an insect or worm, and they will not walk in puddles for fear of stepping on creatures living in the water.

That Artaud died in the psychiatric clinic at Ivry-sur-Seine. He was seated at the foot of his bed. He was holding his left shoe.

Everyone remembers the shoe. It is just the emblem they are seeking. An emblem of absolute desolation and loss. A crazy old man, eaten by cancer, the wreckage of genius— everything is there, the mingling of banality and horror, in the image of the shoe.

The meaningless specificity of the description—that it was his left shoe.

She notices the mug slipping from my grip. She quickly, deftly, takes it back and sets it on the table in front of me. I hold it in both hands. Some of the coffee spills.

I would sometimes carry binoculars on my walks with Roy, to look for migrating birds on the river. I liked watching people also, catching them unawares and unselfconscious. I might look over at a man seated beneath a tree, unwrapping a sandwich or reading or just staring out at the river, and be *fascinated*. I might see this man who is looking out across the water as filled with longing, sunk in despair, lost in reverie, and it was like looking at a painting. I would find myself weaving a little story around him, depending on my mood. I would never, I want to say, just leave him out there alone. I am aware that most people, blinded by their own good fortune and robust psychological health, *stupefied* by the moral obtuseness that accompanies good health and is perhaps its precondition and by the failure of imagination that is its inevitable consequence, would consider my fascination *creepy*. They would consider it a perversion, a criminal voyeurism, especially if they saw me staring through binoculars at an attractive young woman or, heaven forbid, a *child*. They would *not* see observation and study, they would see *ogling*, they would see *leering*. They would be totally unable to grasp the fascination for what it actually is: a waning *art impulse*, one that is steadily failing, that has already *deteriorated* to a distant interest, an interest that is practically a *disinterested caring* for these people whose company I enjoy in this way even though I might not, certainly would not, enjoy having personal contact with any of them.

Yesterday a loud vulgar woman with far too much makeup, a real-estate agent who wanted to discuss selling my house, was allowed to sit at the kitchen table with her *brochures* and talk about that. Even after I had said repeatedly that I had *zero* interest in selling, she insisted on handing me her card. When I refused even to touch it, she put it down on the bench by the door. This struck me as so insulting that I flew into a rage. I tried to throw the card at her as she was leaving, but of course it just fluttered in the air.

For years it was just me and Roy. Now I can be sitting on the bed in my underwear, in the privacy of my own home, a privacy I once thought would be guaranteed by this house on which I have wasted a fortune, and she opens the door to every Tom, Dick, and Harry. The weaker I become, the more people she parades through the house. I lie in bed, sheets pulled up to my nose, glaring, while they tour the house as if it were a public museum.

She has been emptying drawers, dumping them on the table in the dining room. She makes bundles of my cards, cinches the bundles with rubber bands. The dimly lit room, the red wallpaper, the gilt frame of the mirror on the wall behind her: like a nineteenth-century casino, Moll counting the take at closing.

She *meditates* every day, she says. She says it helps her take things as they come.

I was eating breakfast when Alfie let himself in through the kitchen. He crossed the house and opened the front door to the appraiser, the so-called contemporary *art expert* he had hired, and ushered him in, introducing him to me and Moll. A small, slim man with a narrow face, long upper lip, graying hair, and sad, intelligent eyes under thick black brows, he looked like Leo Castelli. With his well-cut coat and tie, he struck me as a *typical* Leo Castelli–type art-movement *imitator*. Alfie climbed on a stepladder and handed the higher paintings down. The appraiser studied them, looked at the signatures, examined the backs, measured and photographed them, then walked to the sideboard and tapped at his computer. I watched from the rocker. They went upstairs to catalogue the paintings there, and all the while, from the moment he stepped through the door, this art expert, this self-styled *art-investment adviser*, kept up a stream of small talk, a continuous patter of contemporary art gossip, the sort of smug insider gossip I used to consume as if it were the water of life, that I used to perpetuate and bandy about in order to make myself interesting, I remembered, listening to the chatter upstairs, and that the investment adviser kept up now in order to inflate himself. I unlocked the studio across the hall, a room I don't go into normally, that I hardly ever go into these days. The largest room in the house, it would normally be the principle room of the house but is instead a storage place for my least significant paintings, a lumber room for art junk. I never go in there. I can't set foot in there without thinking of Meininger, the room made completely oppressive by thoughts of Meininger. Many of his props are still in there—the pink Empire divan, the chrome-and-leather barstool, the antique wicker bath chair, the wooden rocking horse— objects I find myself thinking of as Meininger's *contrivances,* a thick layer of dust and hanging nets of cobweb on them all, the divan practically eaten up by mice. Meininger would paint the same woman over and over, in a manner that was completely obsessive, the paintings differing mainly in the various *fixtures* he would paint her with. On the rocking horse, in the bath chair, and so forth.

The appraiser sat in the kitchen, computer open on the table in front of him. Moll served him lunch, and he ate while staring at the screen. I sat in the wing chair. I fell asleep. I woke up. She brought us sandwiches. Alfie jiggled in the rocker, and speculated about the paintings, repeating the appraiser's art gossip as if it were his own.

We assembled in the dining room, Moll having announced that we should assemble there, telling us the appraiser was now *ready*. We took seats at the table and waited to hear his assessment of my collection, his so-called expert opinion on what I could already sense he considered my amateurish *agglomeration*. We didn't talk. Even Alfie stopped chattering. There was a feeling, a subtle message, it seemed to me, emanating from the appraiser, who was staring into his computer, that we were not permitted to talk. Faced with this professional expert, we had become submissive, childlike, and now he was making us wait. He tapped at his computer, deliberately dallying, I thought, to force us into a state of complete dependence. Finally, looking up at Alfie, he said that *pending more research* he could give us only a rough, *preliminary* estimate. It was, he said, his *educated guess* that the preponderance of the collection was of *modest* art-market value, by which, of course, he meant utterly worthless. *But that said,* he added, looking around at us all, the Lesko watercolors might *fetch a price* if auctioned locally, and the Meininger was an *outstanding* piece. After years of controversy and *crazy* price fluctuations there is now an *art-market consensus* on Meininger, he told us. The painter's numerous late works, while often dismissed as formulaic and repetitive, are *maintaining value,* he said, due to their wide popularity, their use in advertising, and so forth, while his earlier paintings have *stood up under scrutiny,* are now recognized as *groundbreaking* works. The *Nude in Deck Chair* is a *museum-quality painting,* he said, and its considerable value has only been enhanced by the artist's *sensational* end, which has sent prices *through the roof,* he told us, pointing at the ceiling. He was, he said, reluctant to assign an exact dollar value to the painting, given the *notorious* unpredictability of art auctions, but when Alfie pressed him for a ballpark figure, just a *back-of-the-envelope* calculation, he named an astronomical sum. This astronomically *obscene* price knocked Alfie over. He hated the painting, from childhood on he had always hated it, and now it had suddenly become a *valuable art object,* an art object he naturally assumed I would be eager to sell. I told them I intended to take it into the yard and smash it, that I was going to smash it and then burn it. I told them, actually pounding on the table, cutting at the table with the sides of my palms in illustration of my words, that I intended to chop it into little pieces, that I had always intended to do that, that I was going to sell the other two paintings and with the money hire a *wrecking crew* to obliterate the Meininger by chopping it to bits with an ax.

I was overwrought, I was talking in a voice that they all could hear was laden with feelings that no one, myself included, had expected from me. The three of them stared wide-eyed, as if listening to a crazy person.

I am going to stop. I draw up a statement of principles and then I stop.

I will write *Statement* at the top of the page. Or maybe *Statement of Principles*. Or maybe just *Principles*.

It will be Euclidean. It will have theorems, corollaries, and definitions.

Begin with a definition of stopping. Ceasing to move, to think, to want. Desistance. Aboulia. Ataraxia. No flutter of eyelids. No twitches.

The aim is not a definition of stopping, but a definition of going on. Begin with a definition of going on. Or a definition of beginning. Work toward a theorem of happiness, for example. The pursuit of a loved object, for example. Life in that perspective. The loved object: a stick, a ball, or even a sock. Roy was never a fetcher. He could not understand the obsessive-compulsive behavior of retrievers. If I threw him a stick he would amble after it, then just go off into the bushes and chew on it. I imagine he was happy doing that.

I obsessively take my pulse.

She has brought two of her kitchen guests in to look at the paintings: an archetypal neighborhood couple, indifferently dressed in the thoroughly false manner that has become compulsive among people of their sort, a mandatory *casualness* that is at bottom a new formality, as oppressive and obligatory as the old. In just the same way, it occurs to me when she brings them over to my chair to greet me, that their obligatory friendliness is, at bottom, a *distancing mechanism* whose real aim is to make serious talk impossible. They stroll around the room looking at the paintings. The woman says "expressive" or "impressive" a dozen times, the man puts on a show of authority, *pegging* the paintings with art-critical jargon, then glancing at me in search of my approval, as the *owner* of the paintings, and as a fellow *man*.

When they have left I feel, if possible, more depressed than ever.

Unable to pick up the pill I sweep it off the tabletop into my palm.

Walking down to the park, I cross Professor Diamond coming up from there on the opposite sidewalk, walking briskly with long strides, a folded deck chair under one arm. That way of walking was considered "mannish" when I was young. She doesn't turn her head in my direction, and I don't look in hers, hobbling downhill, using my stick. I watch her from the corner of my eye. From across the street I can't make out her eyes, can't quite see if she has sent a reciprocal glance in my direction, but I feel her gaze on me, brushing my face, fly-like. I am the only other person on the street. I am, with my halting gait, my stick, *impossible* to overlook. In order not to turn her head in my direction she is obliged to actively *avoid* turning her head in my direction. This active and conscious avoidance is in essence a form of *staring*, I am thinking. It is staring in a deficient mode, just as her active avoidance is a deficient mode of actual contact and for that reason all the more striking to us both. From now on she will think of me as someone to be avoided, and I will think of her as someone avoiding. In the smooth course of her daily life I stand out as an obstacle.

She would prefer that I not make a statement, I am sure.

Moll in brand-new overalls, on her knees in the narrow band of vegetation between the house and the sidewalk, resting her weight on one hand, pulling at weeds. She knocks the dirt from the roots and tosses them on the pavement. I rap on the pane. She looks up, red-faced and sweaty, and I shake my head violently. She shrugs and goes back to weeding. Half an hour later she is humming in the kitchen.

Scarcely a garden, that weed-infested band of unruly vegetation, but I contemplate it with perverse satisfaction, with what feels to me like satisfaction—a seamless blend of petulance and spite. Though it happens on a regular basis, I am amazed every time I look out and see one of my neighbors in front of his house hacking away at the grass shoots that poke up through cracks in the sidewalk, pulling and hacking at them with small-minded viciousness. I feel completely estranged from people who want to pull grass from cracks in the sidewalk—so estranged that it strikes me as odd I can understand them when they speak.

The other foot is dragging. Two sticks now.

I remember striding, the physical feel of it, the sensation of abundant energy, a plenitude of life, arms swinging at my sides, a spring in my step, air rushing in and out of the lungs as I strode effortlessly. The feeling returns in dreams, as if the body were dreaming. Perhaps I am only truly happy when I am asleep, when the broken body has healed itself in dreams.

In place of the old wooden cane I have two new metal ones. Their length is adjustable and they have rubber tips that prevent slipping. They are depressingly medical, but they weigh almost nothing. If anything they are too light, too responsive to the involuntary jerks and twitches that have plagued me lately, making them difficult to control. I lift a cane, intending to move it forward, and it shoots off to the right or left.

She has brought home a recording of Mahler's *Adagietto*. She plays it over and over. She wants to drive me crazy. She knows how I feel about Mahler, how my emotional life was dominated by him for a long time, how my emotions were structured by his music, how it was only listening to his music that I was able to feel anything that I would call genuine emotion, healthy emotions that were not contrived and sick, and so she is using that music to destroy me, playing it over and over until it is thoroughly trite.

She knows there was a period of life when I was *prostrate* because of Mahler's music.

First it was television, now it is Mahler.

By the time I was eighteen I was already practically insane. By the time I was twenty I was already completely crazy. I must have been partly crazy for a long time before that, perhaps from birth.

I suppose it is still not possible to examine a newborn and determine if it is insane or bound to become insane, though I expect this will become possible in the not-too-distant future.

A note on the kitchen table: "sandwich in fridge."

A young American woman was in a bookstore in Strasbourg, France. It was 1954 or 55. She was very young, scarcely out of high school, traveling alone, it was her first trip to Europe, where she knew no one. It had snowed in the night, the snow turning to sleet in the morning, and she had come into the bookstore to get warm. It was a very good bookstore, with books in several languages, though she did not know this before entering. Now, standing among the books in many languages, she was aware that she was in Europe, that Europe was everywhere around her, and that America, where she had been unhappy, was far away. She thought of herself as taking the first steps in what would become her new life, though she as yet had no clear notion of what this life would resemble. She was at the rear of the store, looking at books in German, though she could not read German, pulling them from the shelves and opening them, because of the magic of the names—Hölderlin, Rilke, Schopenhauer, Trakl. The shop was unusually crowded—people like her who had come in to escape the weather, many of them standing about talking and paying no attention to the books. Among them was a young man, slight of build, handsome in an acerbic way, sharp nosed and thin lipped, perhaps no older than the American girl, though the angular features made him appear older than he was. If the girl had looked in his direction and later written home about it she would have described him as a "European intellectual." And she would have noticed that he did not take his eyes off her. He watched her as she slowly turned the pages of a thin volume she had pulled from a shelf in front of her. She held it almost level with her face and was silently mouthing the words. Though she could not understand the words, she felt, mouthing them in this way, that she was penetrating their deepest, most mysterious meaning. She had often imagined a future for herself in which she would speak several languages and write poetry that would appear in books as handsome as this one. Had she turned her head only slightly to the left she might have noticed the young man. She would have been struck by his appearance, his graceful build (like a bullfighter or a dancer, she might have thought in her typically romantic way), his shock of black curls and his pinched, concentrated features, but she did not turn her head. After a time she left the German books and went over to a table displaying travel guides to European countries. The young man, passing behind her, went to the rear of the store and took down the book he had seen her reading. Holding it against his jacket, in case she turned, he carried it to the cash register. It was only then, when the clerk was folding brown paper around the book to protect it from the sleet outside, that he saw the title: it was Büchner's *Woyzeck*. And that, it seemed to him now, was exactly the book he had imagined her reading. He left the shop. Stopping on the sidewalk outside, he opened the book and wrote in German under the name of the author: "Meet me at six this evening in front of the cathedral." Then he waited. He pretended to study the books on display in the shop window. He stamped his feet on the snow-layered pavement. He was very patient, and very cold. When, after almost an hour, she stepped from the door, his teeth were chattering. He rushed at her, muttering, "Bitte, ein Geschenk," and tried to shove the book into the gloved hand she thrust defensively in his direction. Startled, she clasped the book, but then, recoiling, let it tumble to the pavement at her feet. Overcome by embarrassment, he spun on his heels and walked rapidly away without looking back. The woman picked up the book from where it lay open in the wet snow. She held it away from her body so as not to dirty her clothes and returned to her hotel, where she put it on a chair to dry. Two days later, packing to leave, she was placing the book in her suitcase when she noticed the inscription and slipped it in her handbag instead. She was checking out, and she showed the inscription to the clerk and asked him to translate it. She did not leave that day, and in the evening she went to the cathedral. She had not hesitated, she had not debated with herself about whether to go. Not for a second had she wondered why she was going. She was compelled to go by the logic of a story she was beginning to tell herself, a story that began somewhere in her childhood and ran on unseen into the future in front of her. She went before dark, and she stayed until there was no one else in the street, but two days had passed and he failed to appear. The following day she went again, and a third time as well. On the fourth day she left. She never saw the man again. She never learned his name, but he poisoned her life. The lost *possibility* of that man and the life path he represented poisoned her life. In the core of her being she was constantly aware that somewhere out of sight her true story was unfolding, that her true life path was running on without her. She had many lovers, she had husbands and children. She led a rich, cultured, *cosmopolitan* life. She became wealthy and a patron of orchestras. She even published a small book of stories. But she was always dissatisfied, always conscious of a hollow within. At every check and turn in her rich, eventful life, in the depth of every crisis, she would remember Strasbourg and her failure to open a book until it was too late. It became for her an ever-present *emblem* of loss. She once said to her daughter, "I was given the book of life, and I failed to open it," but the daughter thought this was just a metaphor and failed to understand.

A story is like a path through a wood. It is marked by a series of signs, like directional arrows that say, "Go this way." A story compels us to go that way.

A story is a puzzle in which the pieces instead of fitting together in space fit together in time.

Either way, the result is a picture.

I sometimes imagined, *hopelessly* imagined I think now, a different kind of story, one for our time, that would be the wood itself, without any path through it.

Two packs of ruled index cards. She has placed them on the windowsill by my bed.

I am not so stupid as to begin again. It is only the end that matters in any case, if anything matters. The end, and a few things before that.

Say something before the end.

Two hundred cards will be enough. But if they don't fit together, if the *essential card* is missing?

Nothing but scraps.

A thicket, and no path through it.

We met again this morning. She was walking her bicycle on the sidewalk. I hobbled toward her with the aid of two sticks. We approached steadily. I am tempted to say that we approached *relentlessly*. Gaze averted, we drew nearer and nearer until the bike was rolling between us. A brief thrust and parry as our eyebeams crossed and clashed: I am certain she knows who I am. Perhaps not my name, but that I am, that I dwell opposite and down a ways, that I walk with difficulty, leaning on two sticks, that I am not well.

John Berryman jumped from Minneapolis's Washington Avenue Bridge toward the frozen Mississippi. Onlookers report that he waved. Hapless to the end, he missed the river entirely, landing on an earthen knoll at the base of the bridge.

The jumpers wave.

Virginia Woolf placed a large stone in her coat pocket before stepping into the river.

Ann Quin swam out to sea by Brighton's Palace Pier.

De Staël also jumped. Pascin slit his wrists, wrote in blood on the wall, then hanged himself. Hedayat chose gas.

It is also possible (accounts differ) that Empedocles fell from a carriage and died that way, or fell from a boat and drowned. There were also rumors that he hanged himself. The story of the volcano prevailed. Because it is a story. The others merely offer facts.

True stories are never the best stories, because they lack a proper ending and a proper meaning, but they are the ones that are most faithful to life.

The catalpa is in bloom. Soon the blossoms will fall, covering the sidewalk, and people will have no choice but to walk on them.

Warm, sunny days. The rooms upstairs are insufferably hot, and Moll has brought down her cushion, her *zafu* as she calls it, and placed it on the floor of the porch. I can see her through the kitchen window, a big lump of a woman, eyes half-closed, seated on a cushion on the floor.

She goes about in a frumpy housedress, dark red with large white flowers, a flounced hem, and also something yellow that looks like a sari. Because she is more at ease now, or because the weather is warmer, she has begun wearing shorts. She doesn't seem to care how unbecoming that is.

The two friends I had, whom it had taken me years to meet and finally get to know and become completely comfortable with, moved away. I had inherited them from Meininger, acquired their friendship through him, as a function of my friendship with him. We were all three part of the *Meininger circle*. They moved away and don't write. After Meininger's death they might have written or called. That would have been an occasion to renew old ties, when we could have talked about something else than what Meininger was doing. On the other hand, it is possible that Meininger was all we had in common, that there was nothing else between us. With him gone there would really be nothing we could say to each other. I am tempted to say they should have sent me their condolences when they got the news, but of course they would have been as grief-stricken as I was. That was a feature of a Meininger friendship: you got the impression you were his only real friend.

He managed to give everyone that impression. We all thought, *When push comes to shove it is just Meininger and me against the world, the two of us against all the others.*

The Meininger friendship brought us all together, we became a spiritual collective, but at the same time it set us secretly against each other. We fought for a place by Meininger. The circle was rife with gossip. Like most art circles it was a nest of vipers. If we were not actually in Meininger's presence, we were gossiping.

The initial link, the first intimation that Meininger and I were kindred spirits, was Balthus. I admired no one more than Balthus. I was fascinated by Meininger's *proximity* to Balthus, the fact that he could recount long conversations with Balthus, from when he had stayed as a guest in the great artist's home. He didn't boast of this connection, he concealed it from everyone but me. Our initial intimacy was the shared Balthus secret. In the end I am the one who blurted it out, attempting to burnish my own image through my connection to Meininger, who had been in proximity to Balthus. After that I would systematically bring it up at parties, placing Meininger in a position where he would be forced to talk about Balthus.

Of course with the other two there was the sexual element. I didn't want to see that at first. I didn't want to recognize that their sexual tendency gave them access to an aspect of Meininger that was closed to me.

The closest I came to a sexual relation with Meininger was sharing the same woman.

I woke in the warm, damp bed, in the reeking dark, filled with hopelessness and shame. I was on my knees in the bathroom rinsing the sheets in the tub, it was just dawn, when she banged in and pushed me from the room. I waited by the door, shivering in the cold, the window at the end of the hall growing slowly brighter, until she came out clutching the dripping bundle. I took a bath. I wrapped myself in a blanket and went down and sat on the porch glider. In the early morning silence, every sound was itself, each a perfect whole, each recounting its own little story: the rapid syncopation of two pairs of heels on the sidewalk, the first bus pulling away from the stop; a cardinal whistled, doves cooed. From inside the house, the rasping squeal of my bed being pulled away from the wall.

A tall, obese woman, a woman whose hair is almost entirely gray, crossed-legged on a pillow on the floor.

She has begun posting little Buddhist homilies under magnets on the refrigerator.

I was in the corner armchair reading, Roy asleep on the carpet at my feet. I didn't hear him die. He gave forth a silence, I looked down, and he was dead.

I wrapped him in the carpet, rolling him up inside it. I put the rolled carpet in a plastic garbage bag, and that night I carried him down to the river. I went over the tracks and along the bank and put him down in the leaves. I dug a shallow hole and buried him in the rug and plastic bag and pushed leaves over the grave. I have not gone back to that spot since he died. I suppose other dogs came and dug him up. Or maybe not. Dogs don't eat dogs.

We have reached the end of the experiment. Or as the French put it, more accurately, the end of the experience. The experiment was to see if a creature of vulnerable traits, prey to every manner of pain and suffering, could yet attain a state of calm and serene happiness. The experiment was a failure. The experience has been one of nearly unremitting sadness.

The fact is I am thoroughly tired of myself, of the importunings and plagues of the self, its childish demands and stupid vanities. Self is not a happy man.

Dispose of self one day. Throw him out a high window, stand him under a tree with a gun, feed him something lethal.

Kill it? No. Take it to wherever they keep things like that. Nuthouse. Leprosarium. Institute of medicine, where they can pickle it.

They will say, "His life was marked (marred?) by a series of bizarre obsessions."

No exit. No escape from my enormous egoism.

Even during the final summer, with both of us on our last legs, I would still walk down to the park with Roy, though I didn't throw sticks anymore. He had lost interest in sticks. I would lift him onto the bench beside me. We would sit there, facing the railroad tracks and the river, the city across the river, and the hills beyond that. I would go over the events of my life, the old dead sticks of the past that I dug up and chewed on, while Roy stared at me blankly. Now and then he would thump his tail against the bench to show that he was listening, a bushy tail that he carried with panache right to the end. Learn from dogs, he seemed to say. Every day is all there is. The past does not exist. The future does not exist. What holds past and future together is memory and what holds memory together are stories, and dogs don't tell themselves stories.

A scraping noise from outside. I lean close to the window and look down. This time it is Alfie down there, back to me, bent over, stabbing at the ground with a trowel. I push the sash up. "Get out of there," I yell. He turns and looks up, looks directly at me, wiping his hands on his jeans, and goes back to digging with the trowel. He has dug up the vinca that was smothering the daylilies. He has dug it up by the roots and made a pile of it by the curb for the city to pick up. Now there is just bare earth where the vinca was.

Moll says, "We had blue vinca flowers, now we have nothing."

Alfie and Moll are upstairs, talking as they go through my papers.

She comes down with an empty cardboard carton, holding it by one of the flaps, so it bangs against the steps.

We sit at the kitchen table and argue about the Meininger nude.

Outside in my bathrobe and slippers, I was contemplating my ruined weed patch. I was turning to go back inside. Across the street in the ill woman's house, from the corner of my eye, a crack in a venetian blind snapped shut.

I was not aware it was happening, I would have resisted had I been aware, and now it has happened: a routine has been established. We have fallen into daily habits that have solidified and become inflexible, like an old married couple. We have regular mealtimes. Even the menus are predictable: sausage and sauerkraut on Tuesdays, pancakes on Sunday.

On the refrigerator, in her small, neat script:

Empty-handed I entered the world,
Barefoot I leave it.

My coming, my going—
two simple happenings
that got entangled.

I ask her what I am supposed to do with this, and she shrugs.

The period when I went regularly to cafés and parties, especially gallery parties, when I was an inveterate social-izer and art hound, I think of as the *Meininger* period, even though he was not here for the larger part of it. He was here, physically in this house, for just over three years, and the period endured eleven, perhaps twelve years, so he actually was here for only a fraction of it.

I was leading a thoroughly aimless life before he came. I was constantly on the go. The hysterical energy I brought to socializing, combined with my nearly pathological infatua-tion with all things artistic, made me a minor art-movement figure, I thought, when in fact I was a pathological attention seeker, I see now.

The Meininger period, strictly considered, lasted thirty-eight months, but its effect on my life extended forward and *backward* from that time. As long as he was in this house, whether physically dwelling here for thirty-eight months or being spiritually present for years afterward by virtue of his relentless psychological grip, I was able to look back on the chaos of my previous life, on the active flailing about that was the chief feature of that life, and see it as *waiting for Meininger*. As if all my life I had been searching for the Meininger period.

Almost my entire collection dates from that period. In the process of collecting the paintings I gradually came to think of myself as having instinctive good judgment in matters of art. Instead of hesitating and fumbling about as I had been accustomed to doing, I placed my art bets with the arrogance of infallibility, though the truth of the matter is I was buying whatever Meininger happened to favor, from artists who were part of his entourage.

She rings a bell when it is time to eat. The same bell my mother would use to summon the cook from the kitchen.

Meininger was my friend; for a time he was my best friend. He was not, when it came to investments in art objects, my adviser. He would scrupulously refrain from saying things like, Nivenson (he would always call me Nivenson), I suggest you buy X or Y. Still, I took my cues from him. I would search his conversation, his facial expressions, even his body language (how close did he stand to the painting? was he tense or relaxed? what was behind that smile?). An offhand remark about a canvas, a nod of approval to the painter, and ten minutes later would find me slapping down *thousands* of dollars. In time, after spending a *lot of money* in this way, I confidently dispensed with his tutelage, purchasing paintings he had never seen. As if I could see with his eyes.

He worked by contagion. I walked like Meininger (a swaying, ever-so-casual amble), I dressed like Meininger (white trousers, open-collared pastel shirts, floppy wide-brimmed hat in summer). I picked up as many as I could of his elegant minimalist gestures (slight tilting back of the head to indicate assent, a small slicing movement of an index finger to express negation). He was not tall, but he gave an impression of tallness. His restrained gestures, his handsome, haughty features, his even-toned, methodical mode of speaking (never tumbling excitedly as I did), made him seem an imposing figure. In social situations he was affable, charming, amusing, and at the same time he seemed thoroughly *in command*. I thought of us as pals. Walking down the street or arriving at a party together we were the two musketeers, I thought. It never dawned on me that I was practically his *creation*.

It was Meininger the *painter* and Nivenson the *critic* and *collector*.

The life of a dilettante: a floating, empty life. The dilettante's antics are sincere, without self-mockery or any sense of how absurd he is. He lacks the reflective sadness of a true clown. As a result he often looks like a hopeless bumbler.

There was a long moment between the ages of twenty-nine and thirty-three when I managed to deceive myself so thoroughly that I was almost happy.

She is pushing me in a wheelbarrow. I am in shorts or in my underwear, my naked legs hanging out over the front of the barrow. The ride is extremely comfortable, the barrow sways pleasantly from side to side. She wheels me through a town of narrow streets and half-timbered buildings. I notice the names of the streets: Avenue of the Revolution, Street of Our Lady of Perpetual Sorrow, Avenue of Martyrs. We halt in front of a huge domed building with columns. "This is the planetarium," she says. She upends the barrow and dumps me. I am afraid that I will miss my train, and I begin crawling up the steps of the building, crawling *as slow as a snail,* I am thinking as I climb. I have almost reached the top when I feel myself being dragged back down by my feet, my head banging against the steps, which I now notice are slimy, moss covered. I hear someone say, "He tried to escape." A different voice says, "His shell is completely *crushed.*" I want to see who is speaking but discover that I am physically unable to turn my head. I wake up to find that I am lying cattycorner across the bed, my head hanging off the edge. It is nowhere near morning.

On the refrigerator:

Chao Chou was asked,
"When a man comes to you with nothing,
what would you say to him?"
And he replied, "Throw it away!"

She helps me up the steps, pushing from behind. She waits in her room until I call, then she helps me out of the bath. I stand there, dripping, while she towels me dry. I look at myself in the mirror: a creature of swollen belly, withered scrotum, retracted penis, pendulous breasts like an old woman's, emaciated arms and blue-gray legs, whites of eyes red-veined and yellow, gaze watery, hair thin and arid, skin splotchy, dry, and scaling, nose sharp, bent, bigger than before, a beak. We face each other while she buttons my shirt, a fat old woman and a bone contraption. She follows me down the steps holding on to my shirttails.

Day after day, no trace of bitterness.

All the while I was jotting things down. I would say, "Hold on," interrupting a conversation to jot something down in the little notebook I carried always. I was *ostentatiously* jotting things down. The little notebooks came first. After a while I abandoned them for index cards. The cards were an affectation, I knew even then that I had taken them up for show: pulling from a pocket my little stack of cards, removing the rubber band, sorting through to find the right card, and jotting something down. For years I was constantly interrupting to scribble on an index card. I imagine that a person looking to *sum me up* at that epoch for someone who has forgotten might say, "You remember Nivenson, the inveterate card scribbler."

It became a habit and then a necessity. It is a necessity now. Not for any literary reason, but because it is a habit.

Everything I write on my cards, or on my slips of torn paper, is the working out of a physiological impulse (a habit) and has no literary significance.

The habit of jotting everything down, sitting in coffee shops and bars, or stopping in the middle of a crowded sidewalk to jot something down, made me look demented.

"He was," they will say, "a flash in the pan. He had genius, probably, but it was in fits and starts."

In fits, in spasms. I had regular throes of creativity—*piercings* I called them at the time—when I scribbled furiously. *Now, now,* I would say to myself, it has come, it is here at last. But it hadn't, it wasn't. A line or two, half a page, sometimes only two or three words. It is a beginning, I would console myself, but it wasn't that either, wasn't even that. It was nothing.

It was not nothing. It was a *little* something. A fragment, a scrap.

The deep *metaphysical* appeal of jigsaw puzzles: by connecting the pieces one forms a whole. One *discovers* a whole that was there all along.

At the end of everything—the flailing about, the bafflement, the completely crazy suffering—would stand an impossible artwork. It would show itself as the justification, the point, the actual covert *destination* of the divagations and evasions of my life. Under the influence of the final *impossible* artwork the twists and turns would appear in their true shape as the normal meanders of an artistic life path. Once I had enough cards, once I had enough of the *right* cards, I thought, I had only to assemble it.

The idea that the index cards, which were actually pieces of my life, would ever fit together was completely crazy.

Imagine an expanse of ruins. A vast field on which are scattered thousands of bits and pieces of wood, glass, and masonry. As if a large building had been demolished there, broken into pieces so small and shattered they cannot be identified as window, door, plank, as if the building had disintegrated, though in fact they are not the remains of any building that has ever stood in the field. The debris was dumped there. Hundreds of tons of debris were brought in and dumped for use as building material. But no one has built anything, though the material has lain there for decades, and the people no longer think of the field of rubble as a building site. To them it is just a dumpsite in a barren field.

One day an elderly man comes to the field. He carries a megaphone. He stands in the middle of the field and shouts through the megaphone. The people living in the houses that surround the field come out and stand in the rubble to listen to him. He talks a long time. He tells the people there will not be a building there. He apologizes for not having constructed the building and for having covered a lovely meadow in trash. He ought to stop there. The people have accepted his apology and he ought to stop. But he doesn't stop. He wants to justify himself by describing the impossible building he wanted to put there. He strives to make them see its incredible, heartbreaking beauty. He talks a long time, he is *carrying on* about it. In his enthusiasm for the imaginary building he fails to notice that the people are becoming bored and restless. They are not interested in imaginary buildings and are beginning to wander off. He continues to talk, but the crowd has drifted away and he is alone in the field.

Attempting to pick a pencil up from the floor I make it roll under the bed.

Diamond has written eleven novels, in addition to teaching. Eleven long novels, eleven multigenerational *sagas*, and a volume of literary criticism. The newspaper calls her a literary *powerhouse*. She is a literary *industrial-scale* waste producer. Obviously she is using some kind of *trick*, you can't write that many novels unless you have a trick. For example, the same novel is being written over and over. That is what most of them do. They find a scheme, a trick really, and then use it over and over.

People like Diamond, the so-called literary powerhouses, are the number one *preventers*. Their example, and the malice and envy it stirs up, has been the biggest prevention and barrier of them all, absolutely destroying the aloofness and aesthetic calm I struggled to attain, essentially and repeatedly wiping out the equanimous mental state in which I might have worked with complete indifference. Instead I was forced to abandon that Apollonian indifference, was forced constantly to peer around me, to keep track of what people were saying about me, or what I thought they were saying, to figure out what they were thinking. I constantly had to prick up my ears in order to eavesdrop on what they were saying, and be consumed by rancor on discovering they had not even noticed.

A state of Apollonian indifference—that is the exact opposite of the one in which Meininger worked at the end. Meininger at the end had turned his creative impulse into an exact response mechanism to the vulgar tastes of his affluent public. He didn't have to peer around to discover what they were thinking, because he was thinking the same thing.

"The barrel of a pistol is for me at the moment a source of relatively agreeable thoughts," Nietzsche wrote in a letter.

Roy was part schnauzer and had a moustache like Nietzsche's.

I once put the barrel in my mouth to see what it felt like.

Hemingway also.

When I have the pistol in my hand, I just wave it around.

There was once a story as big as the world. It had a beginning, middle, and end. Everyone recognized himself as a character in that story, knew his place in the plot. It gave meaning to life, though no one thought of it in that way, as having that role, because no one could get outside of the story and look at it. They couldn't know that it was just a story.

"The total character of the world is for all eternity chaos," Nietzsche also said. A consequence of the *failure* of that enormous story.

The world today is everything that is the case. It is the sum of all facts. A story is a *counter*fact.

There are no stories in the world.

The goal, Moll says, is inner peace.

Some things are becoming clear. It is becoming clear that I have to make a stand, for one. Or take a stand, or both. It is becoming clear that I must make a statement, for two. Lacking a statement, it is impossible to take (or make) a stand. Without a statement people have no idea what you are doing. Your statement is designed to clarify that, shed fresh light on it, situate it in relation to its origins, to what you hope to accomplish by it, and so forth. Without a statement your stand will appear arbitrary and stupid. On the other hand, statements minus stands are the sure marks of a blowhard. For me now to make a statement and then fail to take a stand is out of the question.

It was easy when all one had to do when making a statement was offend against good taste, when just making a statement *provoked* a stand. That was possible when there was still good taste, a code of aristocratic honor and after that a code of bourgeois correctness that could be violated. Now they are all louts from the outset. Especially the so-called educated classes, including the local middle class, are complete louts incapable of being offended. They cannot be offended even by good taste. At best they are puzzled, at worst they are amused.

There was once a young woman painter. A young *struggling* painter, impoverished, rejected by galleries, ridiculed by other painters, exploited by men. She kept a diary in which she described the minutiae of her daily life, and it was practically a *book of suffering*. She had made up her mind to kill herself. This was, as she phrased it in the diary, an *irrevocable decision*. There was no imaginable circumstance that would cause her to change her mind. She had even decided on the method: she planned to throw herself from the roof of her ten-story building. The only element of the decision that she left open was the exact moment at which she would do this, that alone had still to be decided. Meanwhile she went on painting, in fact she noticed that she was painting with a new vigor and radicalness. Her paintings, which had been rather conventional and dull, became exciting, even daring. She did only self-portraits now. People who came to view these portraits found them frightening and appalling. They looked at the painter with fresh eyes. Some people thought the suffering faces in the paintings looked doomed. They looked in the artist's face and thought they *recognized* the doomed faces in her paintings. Her complete indifference to public opinion impressed a few people whose judgment was respected, and gradually her reputation grew. She sold paintings to important private collectors. Finally a huge show was planned, where she would exhibit nearly a hundred paintings and drawings she had done during the many years in which she suffered in obscurity. Facing the prospect of this important show, she realized that it was a bridge and that if she crossed it she would inevitably return to being the dull, conventional painter she had been before. She saw that she had to choose between her talent and her life. The night before the opening of the show she jumped from the roof of her building. The show opened on schedule and was a great success. All ninety-six paintings and drawings were sold.

I make a statement, and then I stop. An artistic statement that will make everything clear. As clear as the essential obscurity of the matter permits. A statement about the forest, the denseness of the forest and the impenetrable undergrowth, the absence of paths, the presence of deceptive paths that just stop or circle back on themselves. A statement about wandering off and becoming lost, about thickets. By describing the absolute obscurity, it will make all that comprehensible. An entertaining statement in black and white that will send the audience into paroxysms of tears and laughter and bring down the curtain on the farce.

I never came close to true art.

I was on the sidewalk near my house and preparing to cross the street, when the man backed his car out of the drive and onto the roadway in front of me, blocking my path. He stopped the car, rolled down the window and looked at me with raised eyebrows. I was not sure of the expression, if it was questioning or mocking. The sons had stopped banging their basketball. They sauntered over to the car. One of them seemed to be working his way around behind me. They are behaving like this because they know that I consider his wife, their mother, to be completely insane, I thought. "I am going to my house," I said. The father and the boys exchanged glances. The father said, "Sure, go ahead." I was walking around the front of the car, to get across the street, when he leaned from the window and said, "Do you *need* something?" but I kept on walking. I have never spoken to any of them, not two words, but they can tell by the way I look at their wife and mother that I think she is insane.

Writing up the circumstances preceding my demise, as I have begun to do, though of course not the circumstances of the demise itself, which I must leave to others, I have discovered to my surprise that I am enjoying myself. At the end of a row of gloomy sentences, which I expect will actually *depress* my readers, I notice that I am smiling.

Moll: if you were a dog you'd be always barking.

She has been to the beauty parlor. She has had her hair curled. Her straight, rather *stringy* hair is now a mass of short *frizzy* curls, like an African's. She is wearing pink lipstick.

I turn around, and there is Diamond on the sidewalk behind me, on her way home from the market, I suppose, and walking faster than I am. She will overtake me before reaching her house, I anticipate from her footsteps, from the quick, determined clicking of her shoes growing steadily louder behind me. She is within a yard or two of passing, when I notice the footfalls growing softer. I look back, and she is crossing the street, intending to overtake me on the opposite sidewalk, even though that will mean crossing again when she comes level with her own house, all so as not to have to brush past me on the narrow walkway.

Had I met Diamond at one of the parties I went to in those days, twenty-five, or even thirty years ago, we would have argued. I am certain we would have begun arguing the moment I stepped through the door. The first casual remark, a remark about anything, would have set me off, and once set off I would have demolished her. I would have done my best to completely crush her. I was the sort of vicious party debater who knew how to use every trick in the book, every piece of gossip to crush and humiliate my opponent in front of everyone. I made myself the focus of attention in those days, pushing my cleverness to such a pitch, leaping into every conversation with something cutting or witty, that I must have seemed almost hysterical, I think now. But when Meininger came I found myself stepping back, willingly stepping aside, I thought then. In fact I was being pushed into the background, I see now, *relegated* to the role of Meininger's faithful friend. When I was around Meininger, I felt lumbering. We were often at parties together, and I would come out with some remark that in normal circumstances, I see now, would strike anyone as shrewd or cleverly zany, but with Meininger around it would shrivel the instant it left my mouth, I felt at the time. I would not have finished speaking, and I would see that what I had said was actually flat and completely obvious. And Meininger's presence had the effect that everyone else saw it as well.

I considered myself a harsh critic of contemporary society, a penetrating social critic, and I see now that I was just a chronic complainer.

I lie in bed, eyes shut, while Alfie and Moll talk about television, about programs they both watch on television. I make a noise, it is not a word, just a noise to make them stop talking. They stop talking, I open my eyes and they are looking at me. I close my eyes. They get up and leave the room. Two minutes later I hear them talking in the kitchen. I hear the television. They have raised their voices and are talking over the television.

She has found a wooden cane at the flea market. Now I walk about with two wooden sticks.

I was guided by what I divined were Meininger's opinions, though it is possible, I think now, that he never actually cared for the paintings I was buying, that he might even have hated some of them. They came from his friends, I bought exclusively the paintings of his entourage, products of his *stable* I was already thinking at the time. A few were by people for whom I now know he felt boundless contempt.

I avoided competition with Meininger. Every step I took to evade competition made me more aware of the competition, until we were in constant competition in the mode of avoidance. We started out painting together, in the same house, but in different rooms, and I abandoned painting, gave it up to concentrate on writing, on art criticism, on criticism without rigor that was basically just juvenile poetic *gushing*, that was intended in part to promote Meininger. I compared him to Balthus. The same with women: I stood away from any woman he seemed attracted to. The point was to avoid being defeated by him.

To preserve his friendship, to be together as equals, I had to avoid being crushed by him.

I had nothing to put up against Meininger, against the steady outpouring of those huge canvases.

I see now that I was always afraid of losing him.

We play checkers after supper, sitting at the table in the dining room.

Sunday, and the sound of traffic is barely audible. Birdsongs, mingled voices from the yards of neighbors, the intermittent rhythmic thumping of a basketball. This is life in America, I think stupidly, sitting across from her on the porch. She has made tea. Lipton tea for me in a small cup with saucer, the way I always drink tea or coffee, lifting the tea bag out with a spoon and squeezing it by wrapping it tightly around the spoon with the string that holds the tag. Loose Japanese green tea for her (she informs me) in a large blue mug decorated with a red-and-gold dragon of some sort. She drinks endless cups of tea, always from that cup. She doesn't sip tea the way I do, the way my family did. She holds the cup to her lips and sucks the tea up, noisily slurps it, her little eyes looking up at me above the rim of the cup.

Moll is talking with someone in the kitchen, someone she has let in through the kitchen door. She brings him into the parlor—a man from the newspaper, a large slovenly man with the flushed varicosed cheeks of a chronic drinker. He is interested in the house, she says, and wants to do a story about it. I agree, I consent out of boredom, and I immediately regret it. Sitting in Alfie's rocker, legs crossed, clipboard on his knee, he asks questions that are not questions at all but transparent attempts to flatter me. A thoroughly typical newspaper and media person, I am thinking, who is setting out to weasel his way into my good graces. They cultivate a façade of bland friendliness, a thoroughly artificial *agreeableness* designed to lull their interlocutor into complacency, give him a sense of security, win his trust. They cunningly exploit his solitude and his longing for friendship. They encourage him to let his guard down, secretly hoping he will slip up and reveal some past or future crime or merely say something scandalous or something not even scandalous but that the reporter can twist into something scandalous, give it a racist or sexist slant that the person never intended, in order to make him look like a complete fool. I watch him like a hawk.

Moll serves him coffee, which he balances on the chair arm, clipboard still in his lap. He asks all sorts of extraneous questions about my childhood that I am only too eager to answer. He scribbles furiously while I talk. I haven't spoken of my childhood in so long I practically fall over myself in my eagerness, even though I know I am setting a trap for myself, walking into a trap that I myself have designed, just as I have always done. He asks about the history of the house, of which I know next to nothing. And he is interested in my vitals, the names of my parents, my siblings, the publication dates of my two little pamphlets. He is the newspaper's *obituarist*, I find myself thinking, doubling or even *masquerading* as a so-called lifestyle reporter. They like to have the basic information on hand when it happens, when it "finally happens," as I put it to myself, sitting on the edge of the bed chatting agreeably. What will it say? What *can* it say? He failed at art and life. His death was boring. He lived a long time but accomplished little, anxiety bled him dry. Just a few lines, for those who knew him. They won't use the word *wasted* or even *squandered*, though that will be implied. And of course it will all make sense.

If someone says he is going to tell me the story of his life, I know right away that he is about to lie.

We can't tell our own story. We can't even live it.

If I were to tell Professor Diamond the facts of my life, give her a list of facts the sum of which is the entirety of my life, she would not be able to make a story out of them.

After the success of *The Dream Songs*, not just the public success and the critical success but the absolute *artistic* success, John Berryman must have seen, arriving at the edge of a cliff he had been walking toward his whole life, that he had reached the denouement of *his* story.

It is impossible for Diamond to kill herself except for psychopathological reasons. If she kills herself it will be because she is a deeply neurotic woman. No one will say that she has killed herself for art, and certainly not that her art has killed her.

Moll has gone to a store and bought two plastic deck chairs. She has placed them side by side in the backyard, in the little rectangle of grass and weeds between the toolshed and the neighbor's garage. Sitting at the kitchen table I can look out and see the chairs. Yesterday she sat in one of them, sunbathing in her new yellow dress.

I am not asleep, and I hear her coming down the steps. She stands by my bed a moment, her face in shadow, breathing. She is hugging a pillow. I move over in the bed, and she puts the pillow next to mine and lies down, the mattress slumping under her weight. She stays on top of the covers, stretched full length on her back on the bed, in her yellow dress, and we lie side by side until I fall asleep. I wake up and she is gone.

Meininger set up business in the biggest room in the house. He *jettisoned* all the furniture except for a tattered armchair and a pink Empire sofa, and the room became his studio. Next to it was a much smaller room that I had intended to use as a study and that now became his bedroom. He erected his huge German easel directly in front of the door to that room, turning it into a *concealed chamber,* I thought.

The big sliding doors leading into the studio from the hall were kept shut while Meininger lived here. No one went in without knocking. He had two rooms all to himself, one of them the largest in the house, and he effectively shut them off. The rest of us were thrown together in the remaining rooms. On one side of the hall was Meininger's private apartment and on the other were the barrack-like quarters in which the rest of us were practically camping. He gradually brought in bits of furniture of his own that he used as props for his nudes: a canvas deck chair, a La-Z-Boy recliner, an old car seat, a rattan rocker, all things that I have since thrown out. The pieces he was not using at the moment were just tossed about the room. They were, I thought later, *calculatingly* thrown about the room, to make sure everyone was aware that they were props and not furniture.

The appraiser, when I showed him the studio, turned his head this way and that and said, "So this is the place where he began his famous nudes." They slept everywhere, the famous nude women. Some arrived on their own, but most came with men, with the art bums and drifters who came and lived in my house for years, who *infested* it, I have come to think now. The women belonged to the men, some of them, but they quickly became Meininger's. He painted at all hours, in fits of frenzy. He would sometimes paint for thirty hours straight, bullying the poor exhausted model, forcing her alert, cajoling her into resuming the excruciating pose into which he had manipulated her, and then sleep for twelve. He would get up in the middle of the night, decide to paint, and drag one of the girls from bed. Someone would be lying with a girl in bed, perhaps with his arms around her, and Meininger would come in with a flashlight and take her.

Asleep in the afternoon, I dream of singing. I wake up to the sound of murmuring. I crack my eyes a slit. It is growing dark and she is sitting in the chair next to my bed, murmuring softly. It occurs to me that she is *praying*. She stops when I open my eyes. Looking around, she says, "It's so peaceful in this room now. You were sleeping."

Time is going faster. Everything that has happened, whether it was last week or last year, seems to have happened "just yesterday." With time going faster, everything in time seems to be slowing. Where it once took eight minutes to eat a sandwich it now takes twelve. Time going faster or the world slowing down, as if life were grinding to a halt.

Dizzy after getting out of the bath, I sit on the rim of the tub, calling feebly, holding on to the towel rack. She helps me slide to the floor, and I sit there, my back against the tub. She sits on the closed lid of the toilet. I put my head in her lap. I let her stroke my hair. I feel like a dog.

Awake most of the night, listening to the pain.

Out the window, Moll is chatting with Professor Diamond on the sidewalk across the street. Professor Diamond, trim, neat, *professionally* severe, and Moll in her frumpy smock and flip-flops, looking like a *homeless* person.

I notice Diamond's knees. She is wearing a short dress, above the knees. Her knees are large, ugly, seen from behind they are like swellings, they are like growths one sees on damaged trees. It is wrong of her to display her knees like this, her practically diseased knees, flaunting the fact that she does not give a damn that they disgust her neighbors. Our disgust is a matter of indifference to her, the fact that we are practically assaulted by the sight of those malformed knees.

I find myself attracted to the utterly fascistic thought that ugly people should be hidden away, disposed of in some way. I am completely ashamed of this thought.

The house became a way station for people whose chief ambition was to live an artistic lifestyle, what they considered an artistic lifestyle, which was often a thoroughly middle-class lifestyle minus middle-class *restraints*. They came to the house in droves. They stayed weeks or months. Painters and painters' friends, they came with acolytes and hangers-on, they slept two and three to a bed. They slept where they lay, like dogs, on sofas, rugs, the grass in the yard. I think of them now as Meininger's *art pals*. I thought of my house as a *hub*.

And neighbors also—not my current neighbors, the other neighbors, the old ones who have been driven out, who have been economically *expelled*—used to hang around the house at all hours of the day and night. It was open house all the time, everyone eating and drinking, listening to music, it was like a neighborhood clubhouse. I was a sometime painter then. I was a writer, collector, and also a sometime painter. But it was impossible to get anything done. Even the attic was full of them.

They were pretend artists. Even in the world of minor art waste producers they were thoroughly second-rate. Yet I sought out their company. I can't pretend now that I have done anything other than cultivate such people, among whom I was an *outstanding* personality, practically a luminary. It was my weakness for this sort of company that sank me as an artist. So it was all my fault. Though it was their fault too, for not letting me work, for not respecting my work. It is clear to me now that they never respected what I was doing. Despite their words, they never really believed I would amount to anything, so they were able to get in my way and eat up my food with a clear conscience. Painters, writers, soi-disant artists, using the house as an international way station on their travels here and there around the world, treating it as a food and drink replenishment stop, a free-of-charge art motel, treating me as an art-scene busybody.

I was a small-time patron of thoroughly mediocre producers of artistic waste products, who were eating me out of house and home. And I would think, If only I could get a few hours, a few days, alone, I could get started. I thought about going off to a cabin, moving into the woods. I even went looking for a cabin. To accomplish anything I will have to be alone, I thought. I am a person who takes a different path, I thought, who has put himself through a process of absolute estrangement in order to become a *solitary figure*. I was constantly talking about myself in just such pompous terms, describing myself privately in that way, never in public, knowing all the while how pretentious, pompous, and completely neurotic it would sound. Despite this perfectly solid notion of what would be required of me if I were to accomplish anything at all, I did everything in my power never to be alone, and I basically destroyed myself in the effort, I essentially abolished myself as an artist. Instead of being solitary and deep I became gregarious and shallow. The few times I did find myself alone were the worst. I would fall into a black depression, I would not be able to stand it for long. After a day or two I would drop in on someone, *just for a chat*, I would be thinking, or I would go to a bar or coffee shop for a *momentary break* from the solitude. And of course that would be the end of it. The truth is I was the worst preventer and interrupter of them all.

I did not have a sturdy constitution. I was not a robust man, and as a child I was regularly sick—at one time I was practically an invalid. And I was subject to bouts of debilitating neurasthenia. A car horn or even a burst of loud music would cause me actually to shake. I would be forced to draw back from social life, to withdraw from even my closest friends, and take to my room for hours or even days. If I overdid, if I taxed myself too far, I was bound to be knocked off my feet by a virus. I could not keep up with Meininger. He lived like a dog, eating when hungry, sleeping wherever he happened to be, in a chair on the porch, on a sofa. Meininger, I thought at the time, ruled the night. I would wake in the middle of the night to the sound of voices and music. Meininger having visitors. He had circles of friends that I was not part of, that I felt he wanted to keep separate.

The fact of having other circles contributed to the feeling everyone had that he was somehow inexplicable and mysterious. When one was with Meininger one was always aware that there were aspects one couldn't see, facets that he was hiding. One sensed that he was *incalculable,* and that under the right circumstance he would be up for anything, that he might become *unrecognizable.*

Looking back on Meininger's inexhaustible energy, the overpowering zest he brought to even the simplest things and that put him always in command, I see a man in rags, a castaway of some sort, struggling to climb a steep gravel slope, managing to get partway up and then sliding back down, clawing at the gravel. Though in fact, it was only later, after Meininger's sensational conclusion, that I came to think of his energy as completely desperate.

I resented Meininger, who had not just a group of friends but multiple packs of friends, he had *crowds,* and at the same time was able to turn out a steady stream of paintings, with a flick of his wrist, it seemed to us. He was able to just *knock them off,* even with ten people in the studio talking to him the whole time.

People hung around the studio, on the days he would let them in, perched on the various props scattered about the room. They talked about art, about artists, about movies, and exchanged art gossip while they watched him paint. Sitting around chatting while Meininger worked in silence, addressing each other but actually talking for his ear, they became witty and winning. A mob of minor art failures, addicted to the most hackneyed ideas imaginable, who normally were incapable of saying anything remotely interesting or keen, became clever and attractive in Meininger's presence. In his presence they turned into a *scintillating set,* as if infected by genius.

Professor Diamond, coming up behind me on the sidewalk, doesn't cross the street this time, no doubt recalling the previous incident with shame, her humiliating defeat the last time she came up behind me. With her footsteps just a few yards away, I hold resolutely to the center of the sidewalk, knowing she will have to step onto the grass to get by me. The footsteps quicken—she is accelerating her pace in order to *blaze past me.* And now she is passing, her sleeve swishes millimeters from mine. I turn and look. She is staring straight ahead, her *aquiline* profile inches from my face. I smell the perfume, see the throbbing of the pulse in her neck, and now she is in front of me, in her black half-heel shoes, stepping smartly.

As I watch her walk away the word "hussy" comes to mind. I feel a peculiar satisfaction, as if I have found the right word at last.

Of course this is a game I am playing. A childish, stupid game.

I manage to get the new suit on, a dark-gray suit with vest. She has bought me new underwear as well. She holds the mirror for me to see. She is not happy with the way the pants bag at the seat. I tell her that doesn't matter, since I will be lying down. "Hush," she says. She folds a handkerchief and fits it in the breast pocket.

The taxi driver is a tall smiling African who helps me get in and out. Moll wears a blue loose-fitting dress and high heels. Her ankles and feet are so swollen she has had to manhandle them into the shoes. "You look like Cinderella's sister," I say. I sit across from her in the restaurant in my new suit. She asks me what I want to eat, and when the waiter comes she orders for us both. At the end of the meal he brings her the check. She has *taken me in charge*, I find myself thinking.

She has draped a scarf over the shade of the standing lamp next to her chair, to protect me from the glare. The light shining through the scarf casts shadows of flowers on the walls and paintings. I close my eyes. I hear her turning the pages. I fall asleep, and wake and she is there, and I go to sleep again. It must be left over from childhood, this feeling of peace that comes over me, falling asleep while someone is reading in the room. I wake up again when she clicks the lamp off. I listen to her climb the creaking stairs to her room. Alone in the semidarkness, I watch the leaf shadows moving faintly on the bedcovers.

On the refrigerator this morning, under the magnet that held the picture of Diamond, which I have thrown away: *the secret of happiness is not to grieve for the past or worry about the future, not to mull over yesterday or fret about tomorrow, not to anticipate troubles, but to live the present moment wisely and sincerely.*

Buddha was a dog, I tell her.

Meininger's huge paintings piled up. They leaned four and five deep against the walls of his studio and in the hall. Only toward the end of his stay did he manage to sell anything. Toward the end he sold three or four pieces for a pittance.

The belief, which everyone accepted, which was taken to be evident on the face of it, held that Peter Meininger was a genius. His paintings did not make him a genius, he was a genius before he ever picked up a brush. It was because everyone already thought he was a genius that they took his paintings as *evidently* works of genius. His uncanny ability to sense the newest thing made him look to most people like a genius.

He was capable of becoming a great art failure, I thought at the time. With the critical dismissal and general ridicule of his nudes, he was on his way to becoming an obscure great artist reject. In spite of the personal animosities between us I thought of him as a spiritual art pal, as one of the club. I paid for the paints and canvas. I was *eager* to do that. They were huge canvases, he never touched a brush to anything that was less than gigantic, he painted in the most *expensive* manner possible. Apart from a few odd jobs, he depended on my money, and I fell over myself to help him. For three years I supported him in the most public way imaginable. It was the least I could do, I thought, as a friend of the artist and as a collector. I thought he was a great artist, that we were artists together. I see now that he was a great *sponge* artist.

He had been living in my house for more than a year, when one day he stopped me in the hall. I was returning from somewhere and was taking off my jacket when the door to the studio slid open. He has been waiting behind the door for my return, I remember thinking. He stepped into the hall and gravely announced that he wanted my opinion on something. I remember being struck by the formal, almost pompous way in which he said this. We sat in two straight-back chairs. A huge canvas was propped against the wall in front of us. It was not what I expected. Meininger was a representational painter: despite distortions, one could always make out a figure, a design of some sort, a *plan*, but here there was nothing. We sat side by side and looked at the painting. He sat leaning forward, elbows crooked, hands on his knees, as if about to spring to his feet, as if about to leap toward the painting in order to add some decisive touch. I searched in vain for a motif, an organizing principle: I saw an impasto quilt of ragged reds and browns, a hodgepodge of *splotches*. "What do you think?" he asked. I pretended to study the painting. It looked *unfinished*. Perhaps that's deliberate, I thought. I didn't want to say anything that would suggest it was not finished, if that was deliberate. I was aware that he was looking at my face, at my eyes, he was leaning forward in order to follow the movement of my eyes. I could not find my way around in the painting, it was an impenetrable thicket of color. I felt lost, and I panicked. Meininger stood up. He said, "You don't know how to look at a painting, do you?" His tone was matter-of-fact and dismissive. That is all he said, and he turned his back on me. With his back to me he resumed work on the canvas: I had been dismissed and could now leave. At that moment, walking out of the studio, shutting the door softly behind me, I felt the first stirrings of hatred for Meininger.

Thinking about it later, I realized this this was the first step in Meininger's process of annihilation, his methodical crushing operation, which I would finish up by becoming completely insane.

In the meanwhile, my frank and open admiration of Meininger became a disguise for my repressed loathing of Meininger.

There are moments when death seems to pull back, losing its imminence, becoming just another unpleasant thing I will have to deal with someday. But probably not today, I think, probably not tomorrow, and so forth.

We sit across from each other at supper, talking quietly. The weather is warm, the kitchen door open. I imagine people in the adjacent yards hearing the clink of cutlery, the murmur of voices. I imagine the sounds calling up in their minds images of quiet domestic happiness.

I handed her over to Meininger. I saw he wanted her and I pushed her onto him. It was only later, when I finally got a psychological distance on Meininger, that it became clear to me that I had been acting under his influence all along. He wanted her and he cleverly used his influence to get me to push her onto him.

It was not something he consciously set out to do, he was not the calculating type, he never thought, I am going to *manipulate* my friend into handing over his wife. It all happened quite naturally. The handing over, the voluntary *ceding* of my wife to him, seemed at the time, in the context of the household at the time, the usual thing to do, as banal as the most ordinary commercial exchange. It was a completely normal consequence of the power of Meininger, a natural effect of the Meininger magnetism, of the Meininger *system*.

The system was like a web, with Meininger crouching at its center.

Moll is not well. I sat with her on the porch glider while Janine ran the vacuum. I actively *forced* her to go to Meininger, I can see that now.

In the end I came up with the money that allowed him to start again in California, to go there and move into a first-class studio, step into the middle of Los Angeles art life as an up-and-coming *German* artist, though he had scarcely sold anything. Meininger, the completely successful minor art waste producer, had always intended to become a serious painter again, I still believe. He was just going to *set himself up*, financially speaking, and then he would go back to painting seriously in complete freedom, he must have thought. But that was impossible. In the end he must have seen how impossible it was.

I was always insane, but for most of my life I thought I was normal. I believed that any objective test would show how depressingly normal I was. I wanted to be interestingly crazy. I wanted to be interestingly and romantically crazy, while in fact I was tediously crazy without even knowing it. Meininger, who appeared totally mad, who became practically famous as an artistic lunatic, was secretly a one hundred percent sane art-business schemer and calculator.

I thought he would disappear in California, but he did the opposite of disappearing. With the astonishing commercial success of his family portraits he came to a fork in his life path. This was his second life crisis. He had abandoned his wife and children in Munich to come be a failure in America, and now in California, with his family portraits, he realized he could either fail as an artist or succeed as a businessman. With the unexpected success of those shocking portraits he became a world-class art entrepreneur. He turned himself into an art-genius *impersonator*. Aspects of his character, unpleasant personality traits that he had kept secret from us or that we had dismissed as minor flaws, now became art-marketable *assets*, flaws and assets put on display in the calculated viciousness of his public rants and spectacular feats of self-promotion. The confident and blatant advertising of himself became his life function, and that very fact became a selling point for artworks that with the aid of a *production crew* he was turning out on an industrial scale. He didn't first become a shameless self-promoter in California, but he was now that for everyone to see. And the more he celebrated his own crassness the more he was sought after by a class of people for whom the shameless display of wealth is a way of life.

It was completely predictable that Meininger's portraits of wealthy Californians of the most boorish type, in the midst of their outlandish vegetation and with a background of palm trees and ocean, especially the portraits of their *families*, would make him an art celebrity. An art celebrity who would be invited everywhere as a pseudo bohemian *party trophy*. Posed with the family was always some piece of Southern California lifestyle equipment (automobile, golf clubs, jewelry, furniture, villa), often in the center of the painting and meticulously rendered: this became a Meininger *signature*. They thought these portraits, for which they paid small fortunes, showed the brilliance and comfort of their lives when in fact they were a merciless denunciation of those lives. They didn't see this because he kept to himself, kept who he was hidden from them, behind his affectations, the white linen suits, the omnipresent dark glasses, the crazy stunts. He pandered to them, but I, who knew Meininger better than anyone else, saw it right away, saw the absolute contempt. The minute I laid eyes on the portraits I saw they were practically *homicidal*.

Meininger threw away his genius in exactly the same way that I threw away my small fortune.

He went to California and left me the *Nude in Deck Chair*, and of course all the other paintings. For the past twenty-five years I have lived with a houseful of paintings I was *tricked* into buying. He left the painting here in order to drive me crazy, so that every day I could stand by the

Nivenson mantel and look up at Moll in the deck chair and ruminate about it endlessly, daring me to throw it out, knowing I would not throw it out, that I would sit here in this room and *chew on it*.

With his spectacular, shocking end, Meininger surpassed me even in the art of failing. It was a woman I scarcely know, a person from one of his *other* circles, who told me the circumstances of his death. Talking to people afterward I surprised and shocked everyone, including myself, by referring to his death as an attention-grabbing stunt. It was, I told them, Meininger's last *art trick*.

He had succeeded as a minor artist. His art career was at its peak, with worldwide recognition, when he died. In the art world his death was viewed as a *tragic loss*. It was an *inexplicable* tragedy. The thoughtless reflex explanation one heard everywhere at the time was that he had succumbed to the *pressures of fame*. The fact that he would shoot himself in the kitchen of his own luxurious house, with dozens of close friends, his customers and patrons, partying on the other side of the door, was an offensive and completely shocking display of Meininger's absolute contempt for them all.

John Berryman was a great artist who produced great art. Peter Meininger was a great artist who produced minor art. Enid Diamond is a minor artist, though it is possible she doesn't know that, who produces minor art. Harold

Nivenson was also a minor artist, but he was a *lost* minor artist who was never able to accept his place in the scheme of things.

Her legs and ankles are hideously swollen. Even talking makes her breathless. Janine makes supper. Alfie sits in the rocker and jiggles.

The suicide of Emily Dickinson. The suicide of Walt Whitman, Oscar Wilde was present. I was a child when Dwight Eisenhower committed suicide, with his wife Susan. Hemingway held her dog while Gertrude Stein committed suicide.

What difference could it possibly make?

The Meininger period did not end with his departure. It became the *impossible* Meininger period. Those who remained thought of themselves as Meininger's old entourage, his art pals and his art nudes, but they were actually an unruly mob of losers and failures at every-thing. We struggled to continue after he left. The art-movement atmosphere deteriorated into aimless hanging out. Without him we didn't know what to do with our-selves or each other. It gradually dawned upon me that these were not interesting people. They were thoroughly boring people who had been made interesting by Meininger.

Even basic sanitation became a problem. Filth piled up in an atmosphere of drug- and alcohol-induced *indifference*. At times, rather than wash the hundreds of dishes caked with molding food that were scattered not just in the kitchen but all over the house and yard, people went out and bought paper plates. They filled garbage bags that no one could remember to put out on pick-up days, stacking them on the screen porch where raccoons broke in and tore them open.

The house became notorious as a completely unruly place. It became a house of scandal. I would wake to shouts and see blue lights racing across the ceiling. I spent a lot of money on whole teams of lawyers to prevent it being shut down completely, as an ill-governed and disorderly house, under a statute governing public nuisances. People were becoming sick, they were becoming physically diseased. The atmosphere, not just the actual air but also the entire mental-health climate, had become *mephitic*, I thought.

When Meininger left I went downhill. I did this even though I was recovering, even *while* I was recovering, while I was gradually undoing the tremendous damage he had done. It was debilitating and painful, the surgical removal of the artificially implanted *persona* I had taken on in the course of his period, and therefore it looked as if I was going downhill.

People commented on my outfits. They made remarks suggesting I was letting myself go. In fact I was getting rid of the Meininger style, which for a time required an *anti*-Meininger style, as a form of therapy. In place of the broad-brimmed hat, for example, I wore a ragged watch cap that I pulled down over my ears. I chose ill-fitting discount-store suits even when I could still afford something better. It was psychologically necessary to turn my back on the Meininger *dandyism* at the same time as I was turning my back on his painting.

With Meininger gone I didn't know what to do with myself. I finally locked up the house and went away, traveling first to Mexico, then to Egypt and Europe. I threw away the last of my small fortune on pointless tourism, until I was completely worn out, crisscrossing the whole of Europe, driven from city to city by my hatred of Meininger. In every city I went to I visited museums. I did nothing but visit museums and sit in my hotel. I lived on bread. By the time I reached Istanbul I was completely insane. I had thrown away the little that remained of my fortune and had no idea who I was or what I should do with myself.

She didn't come down yesterday. All day today I have expected her to come down, hearing her footsteps and thinking she is coming down, but she is only crossing the hall to the bathroom.

The smell of incense drifting down.

She has not turned on the television.

Three nights without a light in Diamond's house. She is on vacation, I suppose. She has gone on a trip somewhere, perhaps even a sabbatical. She might have been gone for days already before I noticed. Now I check every night.

In the end I came back. Because the house was here. I came back and found it practically in ruins. The roof leaked and water had caused plaster to fall from the ceilings upstairs. Squatters had moved in, scrawling on the walls and turning the house into a garbage dump. I cleaned and repaired it myself and brought the paintings back from storage and hung them again, thinking I would recapture something of the old life, though of course it was too late for that.

The neighborhood had already begun to change. The social standing of my house also changed. It *metamorphosed* from a center of neighborhood art activity into a place of resistance. It went, metaphorically speaking, in a span of just a few years, from a *hub* to a *dugout*. In reaction, in a reflexive bit of reactive behavior, the sort of behavior I have exhibited throughout my life, where I have always been a plaything of circumstance, I myself changed. From a man in the thick of it I metamorphosed into a *marginal character*.

I became boring. The few people I was still seeing showed by their expressions and by their avoidance behaviors that I had become a thoroughly tedious person, one who was also doggedly persistent and therefore completely annoying. As a thoroughly annoying marginal person I was now forced by them, by that, into what was practically a clinical depression.

That was when Roy came and pulled me out of it.

I went from a socially excluded, potentially suicidal person to a marginal character with a dog.

Wandering the neighborhood in the weeks that followed my return I felt out of place and bewildered. The streets and houses were mostly as I remembered. I found, with minor alterations, the same stores and restaurants, but the atmosphere had changed. The people I encountered in the street were different, they seemed to have a different purpose to their lives, and they struck me as foreign.

Gradually, as the weeks passed, I understood that the neighborhood had been completely transformed in ways that were as yet invisible to the eye. This *metamorphosis,* I came to realize, was like a hidden disease where the death of the patient is already physiologically inevitable even though no symptoms have appeared, where the body, though not actually destroyed, has been thoroughly undermined.

In coming back to a neighborhood that had been undermined, I had not come home psychologically. Psychologically I had actually gone away. If I had died and come back as a ghost, I thought at the time, this is how it would feel.

Moll was not able to get out of the taxi without help. A nurse came outside and stood by the taxi, leaning in and talking to her through the open door, asking questions. Her answers were almost whispered, with pauses while she struggled to catch her breath. They rolled a wheelchair out, and the nurse and the taxi driver helped her out of the car. They walked with her into the hospital, one on each side, each with a hand on the wheelchair, through the big revolving door.

I found a seat in the crowded waiting room next to a young woman holding a sleeping infant on her lap. She was plain, pudgy, and had some sort of eczema on her cheeks. A thin bearded young man in a leather vest, his arms around a cloth bag adorned with cartoon bears and rabbits, sat on her other side. In the seats facing us was an old couple, older than me, who had been chatting with the young people. The old man had begun telling them a story. "It was in Paris many, many years ago," he was saying, "when we were both *impossibly* young." He paused, smiling, while I took my seat and arranged my canes against the chair arm. "My future wife and I," he resumed, looking over and actually *nodding* at the small, delicate woman beside him, "at one time inhabited the same residence in Paris." He talked slowly, deliberately. He spooled his story out in a languorous, practiced way. It was a story he had told many times before, I felt. It is part of his *dinner-party routine*, I thought. His voice was surprisingly young—a fine, baritone, *cultivated* voice. Here is an upper-class, cultivated couple, I thought, who have been placed by this hospital setting on a plane of equality with the young, working-class boy and girl sitting opposite them.

The old man and the old woman, when they were young, he said now, looking directly at me, had often crossed on the stairs of the building in which they lived, and he had wanted to speak to her then but was intimidated by her beauty. "She was a *dish*," he said, smiling impishly and glancing at his wife. He is pleased with this bit of anti-quated slang, I thought, chosen for its *period effect*. Then one day it finally happened: he, on the sidewalk, and she, descending from a cab, arrived simultaneously at the door to their building, where they had no choice but to climb together up the several flights of stairs to their rooms near the top. He asked her how she liked Paris. She said she missed the country. He proposed a walk in a park. She suggested the park at Vincennes. "She said, 'I can make lunch and we can go for a walk in the Bois de Vincennes,'" he said now, lifting his voice slightly to give the words a *female* inflection, *like an accomplished actor*, I thought. He talked as if the young people sitting opposite would know all about the Bois de Vincennes, as if they often traveled to Paris, *including* them on a plane of equality and at the same time *putting them in their place*, embracing them while simulta-neously *crushing* and *humiliating* them, it seemed to me.

The following Sunday they met at the door to their build-ing. What a shame, they thought, to be underground on such a beautiful morning. "'Let's forget the Metro and go to Vincennes by bus instead,'" he said she said. She had done the trip before and knew exactly how to go there by bus. So they took a bus, which rolled a long time through the streets of Paris while she stared out the window in search of landmarks. "Oh, this is the wrong bus," she said at last, and they got off that one and caught another, which turned out to be wrong as well. They traveled to the end of the line on this bus and stepped down in a far outer suburb that neither had ever heard of before. "We hadn't the *foggiest* idea where we were," the old man said now, opening his eyes wide.

Other people in the crowded waiting room were listening to him now. He noticed and talked louder, gesturing as he spoke, glancing around at them all, including them in his audience. He is conscious of addressing a crowd, I thought. He is an incorrigible entertainer, who is now *performing*.

The old man and the old woman (who were young in the story) found themselves in a featureless, gray, suburban district of postwar apartment buildings, small one-story factories and repair shops, with only a dingy café here and there, and no grass and no birds. It was past noon already. Sill hoping to reach "the Bois" in time for a picnic, they walked for miles, becoming more lost with every step, but talking all the while. They came at last to a large divided highway, a busy commercial artery that carried trucks and commuters in and out of Paris. There was a bus stop there on a traffic

THE WAY OF THE DOG

island in the center of the highway, but it was Sunday and no bus came. It was midafternoon now, and they had still not eaten. So they sat down on the hard pavement of the island, and she unpacked her basket and spread out the picnic on the concrete. "We never *did* get to the Bois de Vincennes," the old man said now. He paused, he shrugged, he put on a *disappointed face*, and added, "It was *the best meal* I ever ate," and then he laughed, a raucous, barking, surprisingly *unpleasant* laugh. He looked around at us all. He was beaming, he was truly happy with his story, this completely banal story he had told a hundred times before, and he reached over and pressed the forearm of the woman beside him, who was smiling, and who I saw now was sick. Preoccupied, I had not looked at her closely. I had failed to notice the yellow skin, the emaciated limbs, the discolored wax-like flesh beneath her eyes, which I saw now were actually *sunken* in their sockets. I could see now that she was deathly ill, that it was *her* illness that had brought them to the hospital. She had not said a word the whole time. She had sat with a vague distracted smile on her face while he told the story, which she must have heard many times before, which had become a *ritual* in their life together, I thought. "Don't you believe him," she said now in a small, quavering voice, not looking around but speaking directly to the young woman in front of her, "he has made the whole thing up." "It's *true*, it's *true*, every *word* of it," her husband almost shouted, and they began to tease each other, arguing back and forth about the story, and that also, I thought, is part of their routine. But her heart was not in it—her ripostes seemed *practiced*, they seemed *jaded*. Everyone could see that this small ill woman was truly fond of her pompous, childish husband, that they were in love with each other still, but she was weary of him, I could tell, she had been worn out by him. The young people exchanged glances, each wanting to make sure the other had noticed that the old ones were still in love. They hope to end up like this old couple, to be able at the end of their lives to look back on a *love story* like theirs, I couldn't help thinking.

A nurse showed me into a windowless office and left me there. I sat in a molded plastic chair where a patient would sit normally. After a while I got up and walked over to a poster-sized illustration of a human heart on the wall opposite, the parts brightly colored, labeled, and explained—atrium, ventricle, artery, vein. Arteries in red, veins in blue, with arrows marking the direction of flow. A soft knock, and the doctor entered. He shook my hand. His handshake was loose, relaxed. I recovered the plastic chair. He sat down facing me in a swivel chair he pulled away from the desk. He had tired, grave eyes. A thin shock of gray hair fell across his forehead. A man well into middle age, but his face was as smooth as a boy's. A bland, kind face, I thought. I resisted a temptation to reach out and grasp his hand. "Help her, Doctor. Please help her."

*

It is all arranged. The shipping company has come for the Meininger. It will be sent on to Los Angeles for sale. A young woman and an older man lifted it down from the wall. They swaddled it in bubble wrap and carried it out to a truck parked in the street, flashers blinking. From the window I watched them walk it up the ramp and secure it inside with wide cloth straps. The woman climbed into the cab, rolled down the window, lit a cigarette. The man came back up the steps with papers on a clipboard, which I signed. He tore off my (pink) copy. "Put it there," I said, pointing to the Nivenson mantel.

There is now a blank space where the painting was. The wallpaper there is a darker color, a large beige rectangle above the mantel. There are strands of dull-gray cobweb clinging to it. With the walls on each side crowded with paintings, the rectangle stands out as a place from which a painting is missing, a perfect representation of absence.

I suppose I could write something there, or draw something.

One day in the not-very-distant future someone else is going to live in this house, as generations have lived in it before me. I imagine they will hang something else in the space above the Nivenson mantel, though perhaps not a painting. In the meantime, I am not going to write anything on the wall and I am not going to hang anything else there. I am going to leave the space open, leave it there as a representation of pure possibility, a picture of the future, though it won't be my future. I am not troubled by that thought.

I will arrange the cards. That will be enough.

Sun shining on the saffron fabric that Moll has tacked over the windows lends a yellow glow to the air in the room, which smells of incense still, *like a Buddhist temple,* I think as I close the door behind me. She has taken down all the paintings I had hung there, but left the hooks. Except for the hooks, a little art-deco mirror, and a small print of Hakuin's wild-eyed Bodhidharma taped above the television, the walls are now bare. On the floor below the mirror she has placed a cardboard box and draped it with the same yellow fabric. On the box, flanked by stubs of candles and white paper chrysanthemums, sits a little Buddha made of blue china. A pale sprinkle of incense ash dusts the cloth in front of the statue. Her reading glasses lie folded on a stack of magazines on the nightstand, in a clutter of balled-up Kleenex. Several whitecapped pill jars of various sizes are on the nightstand as well, and one is on the floor nearby. I pick it up and put it on the table with the rest. Her bed was unmade.

Janine has taken a broom and swept the cobwebs from the wall where the Meininger used to be. The leaves have fallen from the trees. The streetlight casts a tangle of naked branches on my bed. If the wind is strong the branches move with small stiff jerks.

The children coming home from school, horsing around on the sidewalk, pushing, shoving, and chasing one another, never glance at my house. They don't see the process of decay. To them it has always been this way, a fixture on their landscape: that old man's falling-down house, as eternal as the moon.

Moll is back. She has grown thinner. She seems frail, her skin has a grayish pallor, and she moves gingerly, as if worried about falling. She cleans less and spends more time in her room. She watches a lot of television.

Sitting in my chair, looking out at the street, I receive little bulletins that testify to her presence: the complaint of floorboards overhead, the rasp of water traveling up the pipes to the bathroom, a burst of canned laughter from the television, footfalls on the stairs, slower than before, the radio in the kitchen and Moll singing along. Now and then she stops in this room. She sits in the rocker but doesn't rock or jiggle. We look out the window and argue about the neighbors.

I don't go the park anymore.

Janine does the shopping. Sometimes she and Alfie bring prepared dishes, and sometimes they fix a meal here and eat with us. Mostly we eat precooked frozen dinners that Janine brings us in stacks from the supermarket, or we order out.

We play checkers.

From my window I watch the giraffes in their Sunday spandex stretching on their little patch of lawn. Ever since I noticed the telltale paunch I have been keeping an eye on the young woman. Today there is no doubt about it.

Professor Diamond's house is for sale. A realtor's sign appeared in her yard last week. They are constructing a concert shell in the park. Moll says they plan to remove the railroad tracks, so the park can run all the way to the river.

The neighborhood is changing.

I was still awake when she came down. I didn't say anything. She smelled of peppermint soap. I lifted my hand, held it so the shadow of a gingko branch lay in my palm. She lifted her hand; the skeletal branch fell across her wrist like a bracelet. She put her mouth to my ear, so close I could barely make out the word. "Love," she whispered, "love." The flesh of her arm lay against mine. I rolled onto her, sank into her, into the big softness of her. She wrapped my bones.

I am going to stop now.

It is not even true that man is born, suffers, and dies. Even that is too much of a story. What is true is that every day the sun rises and sets.

There is not enough time to reckon the sum of our folly.

I am still alive.

COLOPHON

The Way of the Dog was designed at Coffee House Press,
in the historic Grain Belt Brewery's Bottling House
near downtown Minneapolis.
The text is set in Fournier.

MISSION

*T*he mission of Coffee House Press is to publish exciting, vital, and enduring authors of our time; to delight and inspire readers; to contribute to the cultural life of our community; and to enrich our literary heritage. By building on the best traditions of publishing and the book arts, we produce books that celebrate imagination, innovation in the craft of writing, and the many authentic voices of the American experience.

VISION

LITERATURE. We will promote literature as a vital art form, helping to redefine its role in contemporary life. We will publish authors whose groundbreaking work helps shape the direction of 21st-century literature.

WRITERS. We will foster the careers of our writers by making long-term commitments to their work, allowing them to take risks in form and content.

READERS. Readers of books we publish will experience new perspectives and an expanding intellectual landscape.

PUBLISHING. We will be leaders in developing a sustainable 21st-century model of independent literary publishing, pushing the boundaries of content, form, editing, audience development, and book technologies.

VALUES

Innovation and excellence in all activities

Diversity of people, ideas, and products

Advancing literary knowledge

Community through embracing many cultures

Ethical and highly professional management
and governance practices

Join us in our mission at coffeehousepress.org

FUNDERS

*C*offee House Press is an independent, nonprofit literary publisher. Our books are made possible through the generous support of grants and gifts from many foundations, corporate giving programs, state and federal support, and through donations from individuals who believe in the transformational power of literature. Coffee House Press receives major operating support from Amazon, the Bush Foundation, the Jerome Foundation, the McKnight Foundation, the National Endowment for the Arts—a federal agency, from Target, and in part, from the Minnesota State Arts Board through the arts and cultural heritage fund as appropriated by the Minnesota State Legislature with money from the Legacy Amendment vote of the people of Minnesota on November 4, 2008. Coffee House also receives support from: several anonymous donors; Suzanne Allen; Elmer L. and Eleanor J. Andersen Foundation; Around Town Agency; Patricia Beithon; Bill Berkson; the E. Thomas Binger and Rebecca Rand Fund of the Minneapolis Foundation; the Patrick and Aimee Butler Family Foundation; Ruth Dayton; Dorsey & Whitney, LLP; Mary Ebert and Paul Stembler; Chris Fischbach and Katie Dublinski; Fredrikson & Byron, P.A.; Sally French; Anselm Hollo and Jane Dalrymple-Hollo; Jeffrey Hom; Carl and Heidi Horsch; Alex and Ada Katz; Stephen and Isabel Keating; the Kenneth Koch Literary Estate; Kathy and Dean Koutsky; the Lenfestey Family Foundation; Carol and Aaron Mack; Mary McDermid; Sjur Midness and Briar Andresen; the Rehael Fund of the Minneapolis Foundation; Schwegman, Lundberg & Woessner, P.A.; Kiki Smith; Jeffrey Sugerman; Patricia Tilton; the Archie D. & Bertha H. Walker Foundation; Stu Wilson and Mel Barker; the Woessner Freeman Family Foundation; Margaret and Angus Wurtele; and many other generous individual donors.

   amazon.com

To you and our many readers across the country,
we send our thanks for your continuing support.

OTHER BOOKS BY SAM SAVAGE

Glass

$15 • Paperback • 978-1-56689-273-5
$9.99 • E-book • 978-1-56689-273-2

Tasked with writing the preface to a reissue of her late husband's long-out-of-print novel, Edna's mind drifts in a Proustian marathon of introspection. What unfolds is the story of a marriage: is Edna's preface an homage or an act of belated revenge? Is she the cultured and hypersensitive victim of a crass and brutally ambitious husband? Or was Clarence the long-suffering caretaker of a neurotic and delusional wife?

The Cry of the Sloth

$14.95 • Paperback • 978-1-56689-231-5
$9.99 • E-book • 978-1-56689-264-3

A 1999 *Publishers Weekly* Best Book of the Year, *The Cry of the Sloth* is a tragicomic, epistolary masterpiece chronicling everything Andrew Whittaker—literary journal editor, negligent landlord, and aspiring novelist—commits to paper over the course of four critical months. With this send-up of the literary life and the loneliness and madness that accompanies it, Sam Savage proves that all the evidence is in the writing.

Firmin

$9.99 • E-book • 978-1-56689-263-6

"[A] moving and wildly inventive novel."
—*Los Angeles Times*

National Public Radio Book of the Year

Born in a bookstore in a blighted 1960s Boston neighborhood, Firmin miraculously learns to read. Alienated from his family and unable to communicate with the humans he loves, Firmin quickly realizes that a literate rat is a lonely rat.